FOR US

(A Morgan Cross FBI Suspense Thriller—Book Six)

BLAKE PIERCE

Blake Pierce

Blake Pierce is the USA Today bestselling author of the RILEY PAGE mystery series, which includes seventeen books. Blake Pierce is also the author of the MACKENZIE WHITE mystery series, comprising fourteen books; of the AVERY BLACK mystery series, comprising six books; of the KERI LOCKE mystery series, comprising five books; of the MAKING OF RILEY PAIGE mystery series, comprising six books; of the KATE WISE mystery series, comprising seven books; of the CHLOE FINE psychological suspense mystery, comprising six books; of the JESSIE HUNT psychological suspense thriller series, comprising thirty-one books; of the AU PAIR psychological suspense thriller series, comprising three books; of the ZOE PRIME mystery series, comprising six books; of the ADELE SHARP mystery series, comprising sixteen books, of the EUROPEAN VOYAGE cozy mystery series, comprising six books; of the LAURA FROST FBI suspense thriller, comprising eleven books; of the ELLA DARK FBI suspense thriller, comprising twenty-one books (and counting); of the A YEAR IN EUROPE cozy mystery series, comprising nine books, of the AVA GOLD mystery series, comprising six books; of the RACHEL GIFT mystery series, comprising thirteen books (and counting); of the VALERIE LAW mystery series, comprising nine books (and counting); of the PAIGE KING mystery series, comprising eight books (and counting); of the MAY MOORE mystery series, comprising eleven books; of the CORA SHIELDS mystery series, comprising eight books (and counting); of the NICKY LYONS mystery series, comprising eight books (and counting), of the CAMI LARK mystery series, comprising nine books (and counting), of the AMBER YOUNG mystery series, comprising seven books (and counting), of the DAISY FORTUNE mystery series, comprising five books (and counting), of the FIONA RED mystery series, comprising nine books (and counting), of the FAITH BOLD mystery series, comprising eight books (and counting), of the JULIETTE HART mystery series, comprising five books (and counting), of the MORGAN CROSS mystery series, comprising seven books (and counting), and of the new FINN WRIGHT mystery series, comprising five books (and counting).

An avid reader and lifelong fan of the mystery and thriller genres, Blake loves to hear from you, so please feel free to visit www.blakepierceauthor.com to learn more and stay in touch.

ISBN: 978-1-0943-8365-1

BOOKS BY BLAKE PIERCE

FINN WRIGHT MYSTERY SERIES
WHEN YOU'RE MINE (Book #1)
WHEN YOU'RE SAFE (Book #2)
WHEN YOU'RE CLOSE (Book #3)
WHEN YOU'RE SLEEPING (Book #4)
WHEN YOU'RE SANE (Book #5)

MORGAN CROSS MYSTERY SERIES
FOR YOU (Book #1)
FOR RAGE (Book #2)
FOR LUST (Book #3)
FOR WRATH (Book #4)
FOREVER (Book #5)
FOR US (Book #6)
FOR NOW (Book #7)

JULIETTE HART MYSTERY SERIES
NOTHING TO FEAR (Book #1)
NOTHING THERE (Book #2)
NOTHING WATCHING (Book #3)
NOTHING HIDING (Book #4)
NOTHING LEFT (Book #5)

FAITH BOLD MYSTERY SERIES
SO LONG (Book #1)
SO COLD (Book #2)
SO SCARED (Book #3)
SO NORMAL (Book #4)
SO FAR GONE (Book #5)
SO LOST (Book #6)
SO ALONE (Book #7)
SO FORGOTTEN (Book #8)

FIONA RED MYSTERY SERIES
LET HER GO (Book #1)

LET HER BE (Book #2)
LET HER HOPE (Book #3)
LET HER WISH (Book #4)
LET HER LIVE (Book #5)
LET HER RUN (Book #6)
LET HER HIDE (Book #7)
LET HER BELIEVE (Book #8)
LET HER FORGET (Book #9)

DAISY FORTUNE MYSTERY SERIES
NEED YOU (Book #1)
CLAIM YOU (Book #2)
CRAVE YOU (Book #3)
CHOOSE YOU (Book #4)
CHASE YOU (Book #5)

AMBER YOUNG MYSTERY SERIES
ABSENT PITY (Book #1)
ABSENT REMORSE (Book #2)
ABSENT FEELING (Book #3)
ABSENT MERCY (Book #4)
ABSENT REASON (Book #5)
ABSENT SANITY (Book #6)
ABSENT LIFE (Book #7)

CAMI LARK MYSTERY SERIES
JUST ME (Book #1)
JUST OUTSIDE (Book #2)
JUST RIGHT (Book #3)
JUST FORGET (Book #4)
JUST ONCE (Book #5)
JUST HIDE (Book #6)
JUST NOW (Book #7)
JUST HOPE (Book #8)
JUST LEAVE (Book #9)

NICKY LYONS MYSTERY SERIES
ALL MINE (Book #1)
ALL HIS (Book #2)
ALL HE SEES (Book #3)
ALL ALONE (Book #4)

ALL FOR ONE (Book #5)
ALL HE TAKES (Book #6)
ALL FOR ME (Book #7)
ALL IN (Book #8)

CORA SHIELDS MYSTERY SERIES
UNDONE (Book #1)
UNWANTED (Book #2)
UNHINGED (Book #3)
UNSAID (Book #4)
UNGLUED (Book #5)
UNSTABLE (Book #6)
UNKNOWN (Book #7)
UNAWARE (Book #8)

MAY MOORE SUSPENSE THRILLER
NEVER RUN (Book #1)
NEVER TELL (Book #2)
NEVER LIVE (Book #3)
NEVER HIDE (Book #4)
NEVER FORGIVE (Book #5)
NEVER AGAIN (Book #6)
NEVER LOOK BACK (Book #7)
NEVER FORGET (Book #8)
NEVER LET GO (Book #9)
NEVER PRETEND (Book #10)
NEVER HESITATE (Book #11)

PAIGE KING MYSTERY SERIES
THE GIRL HE PINED (Book #1)
THE GIRL HE CHOSE (Book #2)
THE GIRL HE TOOK (Book #3)
THE GIRL HE WISHED (Book #4)
THE GIRL HE CROWNED (Book #5)
THE GIRL HE WATCHED (Book #6)
THE GIRL HE WANTED (Book #7)
THE GIRL HE CLAIMED (Book #8)

VALERIE LAW MYSTERY SERIES
NO MERCY (Book #1)
NO PITY (Book #2)

NO FEAR (Book #3)
NO SLEEP (Book #4)
NO QUARTER (Book #5)
NO CHANCE (Book #6)
NO REFUGE (Book #7)
NO GRACE (Book #8)
NO ESCAPE (Book #9)

RACHEL GIFT MYSTERY SERIES
HER LAST WISH (Book #1)
HER LAST CHANCE (Book #2)
HER LAST HOPE (Book #3)
HER LAST FEAR (Book #4)
HER LAST CHOICE (Book #5)
HER LAST BREATH (Book #6)
HER LAST MISTAKE (Book #7)
HER LAST DESIRE (Book #8)
HER LAST REGRET (Book #9)
HER LAST HOUR (Book #10)
HER LAST SHOT (Book #11)
HER LAST PRAYER (Book #12)
HER LAST LIE (Book #13)

AVA GOLD MYSTERY SERIES
CITY OF PREY (Book #1)
CITY OF FEAR (Book #2)
CITY OF BONES (Book #3)
CITY OF GHOSTS (Book #4)
CITY OF DEATH (Book #5)
CITY OF VICE (Book #6)

A YEAR IN EUROPE
A MURDER IN PARIS (Book #1)
DEATH IN FLORENCE (Book #2)
VENGEANCE IN VIENNA (Book #3)
A FATALITY IN SPAIN (Book #4)

ELLA DARK FBI SUSPENSE THRILLER
GIRL, ALONE (Book #1)
GIRL, TAKEN (Book #2)
GIRL, HUNTED (Book #3)

GIRL, SILENCED (Book #4)
GIRL, VANISHED (Book 5)
GIRL ERASED (Book #6)
GIRL, FORSAKEN (Book #7)
GIRL, TRAPPED (Book #8)
GIRL, EXPENDABLE (Book #9)
GIRL, ESCAPED (Book #10)
GIRL, HIS (Book #11)
GIRL, LURED (Book #12)
GIRL, MISSING (Book #13)
GIRL, UNKNOWN (Book #14)
GIRL, DECEIVED (Book #15)
GIRL, FORLORN (Book #16)
GIRL, REMADE (Book #17)
GIRL, BETRAYED (Book #18)
GIRL, BOUND (Book #19)
GIRL, REFORMED (Book #20)
GIRL, REBORN (Book #21)

LAURA FROST FBI SUSPENSE THRILLER
ALREADY GONE (Book #1)
ALREADY SEEN (Book #2)
ALREADY TRAPPED (Book #3)
ALREADY MISSING (Book #4)
ALREADY DEAD (Book #5)
ALREADY TAKEN (Book #6)
ALREADY CHOSEN (Book #7)
ALREADY LOST (Book #8)
ALREADY HIS (Book #9)
ALREADY LURED (Book #10)
ALREADY COLD (Book #11)

EUROPEAN VOYAGE COZY MYSTERY SERIES
MURDER (AND BAKLAVA) (Book #1)
DEATH (AND APPLE STRUDEL) (Book #2)
CRIME (AND LAGER) (Book #3)
MISFORTUNE (AND GOUDA) (Book #4)
CALAMITY (AND A DANISH) (Book #5)
MAYHEM (AND HERRING) (Book #6)

ADELE SHARP MYSTERY SERIES

LEFT TO DIE (Book #1)
LEFT TO RUN (Book #2)
LEFT TO HIDE (Book #3)
LEFT TO KILL (Book #4)
LEFT TO MURDER (Book #5)
LEFT TO ENVY (Book #6)
LEFT TO LAPSE (Book #7)
LEFT TO VANISH (Book #8)
LEFT TO HUNT (Book #9)
LEFT TO FEAR (Book #10)
LEFT TO PREY (Book #11)
LEFT TO LURE (Book #12)
LEFT TO CRAVE (Book #13)
LEFT TO LOATHE (Book #14)
LEFT TO HARM (Book #15)
LEFT TO RUIN (Book #16)

THE AU PAIR SERIES
ALMOST GONE (Book#1)
ALMOST LOST (Book #2)
ALMOST DEAD (Book #3)

ZOE PRIME MYSTERY SERIES
FACE OF DEATH (Book#1)
FACE OF MURDER (Book #2)
FACE OF FEAR (Book #3)
FACE OF MADNESS (Book #4)
FACE OF FURY (Book #5)
FACE OF DARKNESS (Book #6)

A JESSIE HUNT PSYCHOLOGICAL SUSPENSE SERIES
THE PERFECT WIFE (Book #1)
THE PERFECT BLOCK (Book #2)
THE PERFECT HOUSE (Book #3)
THE PERFECT SMILE (Book #4)
THE PERFECT LIE (Book #5)
THE PERFECT LOOK (Book #6)
THE PERFECT AFFAIR (Book #7)
THE PERFECT ALIBI (Book #8)
THE PERFECT NEIGHBOR (Book #9)
THE PERFECT DISGUISE (Book #10)

THE PERFECT SECRET (Book #11)
THE PERFECT FAÇADE (Book #12)
THE PERFECT IMPRESSION (Book #13)
THE PERFECT DECEIT (Book #14)
THE PERFECT MISTRESS (Book #15)
THE PERFECT IMAGE (Book #16)
THE PERFECT VEIL (Book #17)
THE PERFECT INDISCRETION (Book #18)
THE PERFECT RUMOR (Book #19)
THE PERFECT COUPLE (Book #20)
THE PERFECT MURDER (Book #21)
THE PERFECT HUSBAND (Book #22)
THE PERFECT SCANDAL (Book #23)
THE PERFECT MASK (Book #24)
THE PERFECT RUSE (Book #25)
THE PERFECT VENEER (Book #26)
THE PERFECT PEOPLE (Book #27)
THE PERFECT WITNESS (Book #28)
THE PERFECT APPEARANCE (Book #29)
THE PERFECT TRAP (Book #30)
THE PERFECT EXPRESSION (Book #31)

CHLOE FINE PSYCHOLOGICAL SUSPENSE SERIES
NEXT DOOR (Book #1)
A NEIGHBOR'S LIE (Book #2)
CUL DE SAC (Book #3)
SILENT NEIGHBOR (Book #4)
HOMECOMING (Book #5)
TINTED WINDOWS (Book #6)

KATE WISE MYSTERY SERIES
IF SHE KNEW (Book #1)
IF SHE SAW (Book #2)
IF SHE RAN (Book #3)
IF SHE HID (Book #4)
IF SHE FLED (Book #5)
IF SHE FEARED (Book #6)
IF SHE HEARD (Book #7)

THE MAKING OF RILEY PAIGE SERIES
WATCHING (Book #1)

WAITING (Book #2)
LURING (Book #3)
TAKING (Book #4)
STALKING (Book #5)
KILLING (Book #6)

RILEY PAIGE MYSTERY SERIES
ONCE GONE (Book #1)
ONCE TAKEN (Book #2)
ONCE CRAVED (Book #3)
ONCE LURED (Book #4)
ONCE HUNTED (Book #5)
ONCE PINED (Book #6)
ONCE FORSAKEN (Book #7)
ONCE COLD (Book #8)
ONCE STALKED (Book #9)
ONCE LOST (Book #10)
ONCE BURIED (Book #11)
ONCE BOUND (Book #12)
ONCE TRAPPED (Book #13)
ONCE DORMANT (Book #14)
ONCE SHUNNED (Book #15)
ONCE MISSED (Book #16)
ONCE CHOSEN (Book #17)

MACKENZIE WHITE MYSTERY SERIES
BEFORE HE KILLS (Book #1)
BEFORE HE SEES (Book #2)
BEFORE HE COVETS (Book #3)
BEFORE HE TAKES (Book #4)
BEFORE HE NEEDS (Book #5)
BEFORE HE FEELS (Book #6)
BEFORE HE SINS (Book #7)
BEFORE HE HUNTS (Book #8)
BEFORE HE PREYS (Book #9)
BEFORE HE LONGS (Book #10)
BEFORE HE LAPSES (Book #11)
BEFORE HE ENVIES (Book #12)
BEFORE HE STALKS (Book #13)
BEFORE HE HARMS (Book #14)

AVERY BLACK MYSTERY SERIES
CAUSE TO KILL (Book #1)
CAUSE TO RUN (Book #2)
CAUSE TO HIDE (Book #3)
CAUSE TO FEAR (Book #4)
CAUSE TO SAVE (Book #5)
CAUSE TO DREAD (Book #6)

KERI LOCKE MYSTERY SERIES
A TRACE OF DEATH (Book #1)
A TRACE OF MURDER (Book #2)
A TRACE OF VICE (Book #3)
A TRACE OF CRIME (Book #4)
A TRACE OF HOPE (Book #5)

PROLOGUE

The stage lights shone brightly, casting a warm glow on Lizzie's skin as she took her final step forward. She knew her smile was wide and inviting, with the confidence of a born performer; she'd practiced it endlessly in the mirror earlier. The audience erupted into applause, their cheers an intoxicating affirmation of her hard work and dedication.

"Thank you!" she called out, waving to the sea of faces before her. The blinding lights made it difficult to see anyone in particular, but that didn't matter. Right now, this moment was hers, and she soaked it in like a sponge.

As soon as she exited the stage, Lizzie hurried down the dimly lit hallway toward her dressing room. The sound of the audience's approval still echoed in her ears, but it had already begun to fade. She could feel her heart pounding in her chest, the adrenaline wearing off as reality began to set back in.

The moment she set foot in her dressing room, Lizzie allowed her smile to fall away like a discarded mask. The room seemed smaller than before, the familiar scents of makeup and hairspray failing to bring her any comfort. With each step closer to the mirror, Lizzie felt more and more like a stranger in her own body.

"Alright, Lizzie," she whispered to herself, staring at her reflection. "You did it. Now just breathe."

Lizzie's chest heaved as she let out a shaky breath, her legs giving way beneath her. She collapsed into the plush chair in the corner of her dressing room, feeling the weight of the performance bear down on her. A cold sweat dampened her skin, and she could already feel the encroaching threat of anxiety clawing at the edges of her mind.

Did I... did I mess up? she wondered to herself. Her hands trembled, clasped tightly together in her lap. *No, no, Lizzie, you were great,* she tried to reassure herself, but doubt gnawed at her heart like a ravenous beast.

Her mind raced as she replayed every minute of her act, meticulously dissecting each moment with merciless scrutiny. The graceful twirl that felt slightly off-balance, the brief, almost imperceptible hesitation before launching into her final pose. Each perceived flaw amplified until it consumed her thoughts, obliterating any trace of triumph that had lingered from the applause.

"Stop it!" she muttered through gritted teeth, tears pricking at the corners of her eyes. But her mind refused to relent, dragging her deeper and deeper into the relentless storm of self-doubt. "Five, six, seven, eight," she muttered frantically, her fingers tapping out the rhythm against her thigh as if trying to physically banish the mistake from existence. "I knew I should've practiced more."

Her tear-filled gaze locked onto her reflection in the mirror. *You're a wreck, Lizzie. Just because you didn't nail that one move doesn't mean it's all over.* Her own words of encouragement sounded hollow and unconvincing, even to herself.

Maybe they didn't notice, she reasoned, desperately clinging to the hope that the audience had been too captivated by her performance to spot any errors. But the thought brought little comfort, for she knew that she would always be haunted by the knowledge of her imperfections.

As Lizzie sank further into her thoughts, she couldn't help but feel as though she were teetering on the edge of some dark abyss. The pressure and expectations she had placed upon herself threatened to swallow her whole, leaving nothing behind but a hollow shell of who she used to be. And yet, in the depths of her despair, there was one thing that remained certain: she would not let this moment define her. She might stumble and falter, but she would keep pushing forward, striving to become the best version of herself.

"Come on, Lizzie," she whispered, her voice wavering. "You're stronger than this."

Just then, a faint creaking sound drew her attention away from the mirror. Lizzie's heart skipped a beat as she turned towards the source of the noise. In that split second, the dressing room door flew open and a man emerged from the shadows, brandishing a gun.

"Don't you dare scream," he hissed, his voice low and menacing.

Lizzie's eyes widened in terror, her breath catching in her throat. She instinctively raised her hands in surrender, unable to comprehend what was happening.

"Wh-what do you want?" she stammered, her voice barely audible.

"Move. Follow me. And stay quiet," he ordered, his cold gaze never leaving her face. "I know about your secret, Lizzie."

Her stomach churned at the mention of her secret, but she knew she couldn't let him see her fear. She nodded silently, trying to keep her breathing steady, but the questions kept coming. Who was this man? How did he know her secret?

And most importantly, what did he plan to do with her?

"Walk," he commanded, gesturing towards the door with the gun.

With no other choice, Lizzie forced herself to take one shaky step, then another, feeling the weight of the gun pressing into her back like an icy blade. Her thoughts swirled chaotically, searching for any way out of this nightmare. But deep down, she knew that there was no escape, not when her darkest secret was on the line. She'd rather die than let it be exposed.

"Keep moving," the man growled, his impatience evident in the tightness of his grip on the weapon.

As they made their way through dimly lit corridors, Lizzie tried to memorize their path, her mind working overtime to formulate a plan. She knew she had to act fast before it was too late. But for now, she could only follow the man's orders and hope that an opportunity would present itself.

"Where are you taking me?" she asked, her voice trembling with fear and anger. "Why are you doing this?"

"Shut up," he snapped, giving her a shove forward. "You'll find out soon enough."

They found their way to the exit, and Lizzie felt as though she were stepping closer to her doom with every step. The air outside was heavy with humidity, clinging to Lizzie's skin like a film. It was so dark that she could barely see the street in front of her. The gun pressed against her back was a constant reminder of the precariousness of her situation, yet it also fueled her determination to find a way out. But could there be a way out?

"Turn left here," the man commanded, his voice low and menacing. Lizzie obeyed, feeling the damp pavement beneath her feet as they entered a narrow, dimly lit alleyway. The scent of rotting garbage filled her nostrils, and she tried not to gag.

"Can't you tell me what you want?" Lizzie asked, her voice quivering. She hated herself for showing her fear, but she couldn't help it.

"Didn't I tell you to shut up?" the man snapped, giving her another shove forward. "You'll know soon enough."

Lizzie bit her lip, swallowing down the terror that threatened to consume her. As they continued to walk, she noticed a broken bottle on the ground, its jagged edges reflecting what little light there was. A desperate idea began to form in her mind.

"Please," she whispered, forcing herself to sound as pathetic as possible. "I can't go any further. My feet hurt so much."

"Keep moving," the man growled, his breath hot on her neck.

"Where are you taking me?" Lizzie whispered, her voice barely audible.

"Shut up."

Lizzie clenched her jaw, focusing on each step as she tried to calm her racing thoughts. She knew she couldn't call for help; there was too much at risk. Instead, she had to rely on herself and find a way out of this nightmare.

As they continued through the alley, Lizzie's eyes darted around, searching for anything she could use to her advantage. Broken glass glinted on the ground, graffiti-covered walls closed in on either side, and the distant hum of city life taunted her with its normalcy. But there was nothing she could do.

They got to the end of the alleyway, and the man said, "Turn around."

Lizzie faced him, her heart in her throat. His face was obscured by shadow. Shakily, he handed her a pair of gloves.

"Put these on," he said.

"W-what?" Lizzie stammered.

"I said *put them on!*" he snarled, and Lizzie instantly did as she was told. She put the gloves on, and something wet instantly hit her palms within them. A strange, chemical smell filled her nostrils.

"Good," the man said, a smile playing at the bottom half of his face. "Now, place your hands together."

Lizzie did as she was told and placed her hands together, the substance on the gloves quickly gluing them together. She tried to pull them apart, but it was no use. Panic flooded through her veins.

"What... What did you do?" she asked, her voice trembling with fear.

The man's smile widened as he spoke. "You'll find out soon," he said calmly. "I could have killed you there and then, but I think this is more fun."

A sudden feeling of sickness began to make its way through Lizzie's body, her heart pounding and her stomach lurching, her skin sweating unnaturally. The man's smile only widened as Lizzie realized what had happened--

Putting these gloves on had sealed her fate.

The poison was working, and soon, she'd be dead.

CHAPTER ONE

The sun filtered through the canopy of trees as Special Agent Morgan Cross drove her car down a winding path in the forest. Midday light danced around her, casting dappled shadows on the dashboard. The hum of the engine provided a steady rhythm to her thoughts, and for a moment, she allowed herself to escape the harsh realities of her life.

"Almost there, Skunk," she murmured, glancing at the rearview mirror where her faithful Pitbull sat, panting happily and wagging his tail. His unwavering loyalty was a comfort to her, especially after everything she had been through.

"Hard to believe it's been so long, huh?" she said to Skunk, her voice tinged with melancholy. Memories of her time in prison still haunted her, the injustice of being framed for murder weighing heavily on her soul. Morgan had been out for months now after ten years behind bars after she was framed for being an accomplice to Samson, the Seven Signs Killer. But when Samson came back, the truth all came out, and the media—and *some* members of the FBI—took Morgan's side.

She had been reinstated as an agent, but it wasn't without her own personal gripes. Now, after everything she'd been through since getting out of prison, she knew that she had been framed by someone with connections to the FBI. It was still unclear to her who, but it seemed to have something to do with her father. Morgan had never known her father to be an FBI agent before he died, and Morgan had seen the picture of him with other agents, years ago, before Morgan was even born...

If the photo was indeed real, then there was so much about her own past that Morgan didn't know. But that was why she was here--to hopefully find some answers.

The tires crunched over gravel as they finally arrived at the cabin, its wooden façade blending seamlessly into the surrounding foliage. It had belonged to her father.

"Maybe we'll find some answers here, buddy," she whispered, more to herself than to Skunk. Morgan needed this break from her duties at the FBI, hoping that it would offer her the chance to delve into her past and unravel the enigma that was her father.

Morgan's hand hovered over the ignition as she stared at the quaint wooden cabin nestled among the trees. Her mind raced with questions that refused to be silenced. Why had her father never mentioned his time with the FBI?

"Can't believe he never told me," she muttered under her breath, her grip on the steering wheel tightening. Skunk whined from the backseat, sensing her unease. Morgan took a deep breath, forcing herself to focus on the present moment. "Alright, let's do this, buddy."

She stepped out of the car and into the dappled sunlight that filtered through the swaying branches above. Instantly, memories of summers spent with her father flooded back, each one a bittersweet reminder of simpler times. Here, she had learned how to fish in the nearby stream, and how to track deer through the dense undergrowth. It was also where she first discovered her love for reading, devouring every book she could get her hands on.

"Remember this place, Skunk?" she asked, glancing back at her faithful companion as he eagerly sniffed around the cabin's perimeter. He looked up at her and wagged his tail before resuming his investigation.

"Used to spend hours just sitting on the porch with Dad, talking about anything and everything," she said quietly, her voice thick with emotion. "I always felt close to him here, like I could share anything with him. But it seems I didn't know him as well as I thought."

Skunk trotted back to her side, pressing his warm body against her leg in silent support. Morgan gave him a grateful pat on the head before turning her attention back to the cabin. It was time to do this.

Morgan hefted her luggage from the trunk, the weight of it a reminder of the emotional baggage she carried with her. Skunk whined at her side, as if sensing her unease, and she gave him a reassuring pat before trudging toward the cabin.

The wooden porch creaked underfoot as Morgan approached the door, an old-fashioned keyring clenched tightly in her hand. She inserted the key into the lock, her pulse quickening at the thought of what secrets the cabin might hold. With a faint click, the door swung open, revealing a world she had left behind long ago.

"Ugh," she grunted, stepping inside and immediately recoiling at the smell of stale air and dust. "This place could use a good cleaning."

Her dad would have been the last one here, she mused, surveying the musty interior. The furniture was draped in white sheets, untouched since her father's death. She hadn't been here since her release from prison, and the realization weighed on her heart like a stone.

Skunk bounded in after her, his nails tapping on the wooden floor as he happily sniffed his surroundings. Morgan set her luggage down with a sigh and looked around, her eyes suddenly filling with tears.

Everywhere she looked, memories came flooding back: family photos adorning the walls, her father's prized shotgun mounted above the fireplace, her mother's extensive collection of books lining the shelves.

Seems like a lifetime ago. Morgan sighed, wiping away a stray tear. She knew she couldn't afford to get lost in memories; there was work to be done.

Morgan's fingers grazed the spines of her mother's books as she scanned the titles, searching for any clue that might help her unravel the mystery of her father's past. A floorboard creaked behind her, and Skunk's low growl sent a shiver down her spine.

"Skunk, what is it?" she asked, her voice barely above a whisper. The Pitbull's ears were pricked forward, his body tense, and his eyes locked on the window.

"Is someone out there?" Morgan's heart raced, and she instinctively reached for her father's shotgun mounted above the fireplace. She checked to make sure it was loaded before carefully making her way to the door, Skunk following close behind.

As she stepped outside, the crisp air hit her face, only heightening her senses as she surveyed the surrounding woods.

"Hello? Is anyone there?" Her voice echoed through the trees, but there was no response. Skunk continued to bark and whine, his tail tucked between his legs. Morgan squinted into the shadows, her hands gripping the shotgun tightly, ready for anything.

"Come on, Skunk. It's probably just an animal," she muttered, trying to convince herself more than the dog. But deep down, she couldn't shake the feeling that they weren't alone. She knew better than most that danger could lurk in the most unexpected places.

Just as Morgan was about to retreat back inside, a deer emerged from the bush, its large dark eyes meeting hers for a brief moment before it bounded away gracefully. She let out a sigh of relief and lowered her gun, her heart still pounding in her chest.

"Alright, boy, settle down," she commanded Skunk, who whined but obeyed, his tense posture relaxing. Together, they went back inside the cabin, and Morgan locked the door behind them, vowing to be more vigilant than ever during their stay.

"See, Skunk? Just a deer," she said, trying to reassure both herself and the dog. "Nothing to worry about." Still, she couldn't help but feel a lingering unease as she stood in the quiet cabin, her father's presence looming over her like a ghost.

***

Later that night, Morgan sat on the worn couch, her fingers wrapped around a glass of scotch, savoring the slow burn as it slid down her throat. The fire crackled in the fireplace, casting flickering shadows on the walls, and Skunk lay curled up at her feet, snoring softly.

In her lap were several old photo albums she had found in her father's room, their pages filled with memories she had tried so hard to forget. As she flipped through the photographs, Morgan couldn't help but feel a sharp pang of longing for the simpler times depicted within them - summers spent fishing and exploring the woods, her mother's laughter ringing through the air, her father teaching her how to shoot a gun.

"God, Dad, what secrets were you keeping?" she whispered, her voice barely audible above the crackling fire. There had to be something here, some clue as to why her father had hidden his past as an FBI agent from her. But so far, all she had found were family memories and mementos of a life she no longer recognized.

Maybe it was all bullshit anyway. After all, it had been Derik who had left her the photo of her dad… a way to trick her, on behalf of the men who had tried to frame her, who were leveraging Derik's son. Maybe it was an edited photo, but as much as Morgan didn't trust Derik, she didn't see the point in him lying to her about this one. Maybe she was a fool for believing the story about his son, but…

As much as Derik had betrayed her, he had still been a close friend for well over a decade. Even when she was in prison…

Morgan took another sip of her scotch, the warmth offering little comfort against the chill that had settled over her. She glanced around the cabin, unease still lingering in the pit of her stomach. The feeling that they were being watched hadn't entirely dissipated, and she wondered if it was her own paranoia or something more ominous at play.

Morgan's fingers traced the worn edges of a photograph, her eyes drinking in the image of herself as a child, standing beside her beaming mother. The warmth of the memory tugged at her heart, but she couldn't shake the sinking feeling that there was something missing - something vital.

"Nothing about the FBI," she muttered, frustration mounting as she flipped through page after page of family vacations, holiday celebrations, and everyday life. "Where are you hiding your secrets, Dad?"

Skunk shifted on the floor beside her, his soft snores a comforting presence in the otherwise silent cabin. Morgan glanced around, the shadows cast by the flickering firelight making her skin crawl. It felt as if someone was watching her, an unseen presence just outside her line of sight. But even as she tried to resume her search, her thoughts turned back to the strange sensation of being watched. She couldn't ignore it any longer.

"Skunk, stay here," she instructed, her voice low and steady as she rose from her seat. The Pitbull lifted his head, his dark eyes following her movements with concern.

She moved quickly through the cabin, pulling the curtains closed with a swiftness born of years spent looking over her shoulder. As each window was covered, a small part of her mind protested that she was being paranoid, that there was no one out there. But another, more primal instinct urged her to take precautions, to remain vigilant against the darkness that seemed to press in from all sides. And the truth was, she felt better with all the curtains closed.

Morgan sank back into the worn cushions of the couch, her fingers absently tracing the edge of the glass tumbler in her hand. The amber liquid inside sloshed gently as she stared into the dancing flames of the fireplace, their warmth casting flickering shadows across the dimly lit room.

As she tried to focus, thoughts of her partner, Derik Greene, snuck back into her mind. It was Derik who had betrayed her trust, working with the people who had possibly framed Morgan, attempting to trick her and get rid of her a second time. But Morgan knew now that they had something on Derik--his son, who even Morgan hadn't known about. She understood Derik's plight, and in the end, he had risked everything to inform Morgan that she had been walking into a trap.

It only confused her more. Morgan still didn't trust Derik. He still hadn't informed her who these men could be, but it was entirely possible that he truly didn't know. Derik was a pawn to them too...

"Damn you, Derik," she murmured, allowing herself a moment to think about her partner. Betrayal was an all-too-familiar companion in her life, but somehow, Derik's had stung more than most. She'd trusted him – perhaps even cared for him – and he'd lied to her. She swished the scotch around her glass before taking another slow sip. Her thoughts drifted back over the past year, remembering the countless cases they'd solved together, the late nights spent poring over files and evidence in search of justice for the victims. He'd become more than just a partner; he'd been her friend. And now... what? Could she ever trust him again?

"Skunk, what do you think?" she asked softly, glancing down at the Pitbull, who lay curled up beside her. His dark eyes met hers, offering nothing but loyalty and understanding. "Can I really trust him after everything?"

The dog let out a low whine, his gaze never leaving hers.

Morgan sighed, shaking her head. "You're right," she agreed, trying to ignore the raw ache in her chest. "I can't afford to be foolish."

She took another drink, the burn of the scotch chasing away some of the cold that seeped into her bones. For a moment, she allowed herself to imagine what it would be like to let someone in again, to open herself up to the possibility of trust. But the memories of betrayal, of prison bars and shattered dreams, were too strong. She couldn't risk it.

"Never again," she whispered, her voice barely audible above the crackling fire. She drained the last of the scotch from her glass, her eyelids growing heavy as the warmth of the alcohol spread through her body. Sleep slowly overtook her, pulling her down into its dark embrace as she lay there on the couch, the ghost of Derik's betrayal still haunting her thoughts.

Skunk shifted closer to her side, his warm body a solid presence against the chill of the night air. Together, they slipped into a restless slumber, the shadows in the cabin offering no comfort or solace to either of them.

CHAPTER TWO

The next day, the aroma of sizzling onions and garlic filled the cabin's modest kitchen as Morgan busied herself with chopping tomatoes and bell peppers for her spaghetti dinner. While she was no culinary expert, she found a certain solace in the rhythmic act of cooking, the way it demanded just enough focus to keep her thoughts from straying too far into the darkness that always seemed to linger at the edges of her mind. She'd slept poorly last night, but that was nothing new, and had spent the entire day chopping wood and going through her father's belongings. So far, she'd found nothing of importance, only memories.

Skunk lay on the floor nearby, his eyes tracking her every movement with an eager intensity that suggested he was hoping for a dropped morsel or two. She smiled down at him, grateful for the simple, uncomplicated love he offered.

"Maybe I ought to teach you how to cook," she joked, tossing him a scrap of chicken that he caught mid-air. "Then I could put my feet up and relax for a change."

Just as she was reaching for the salt, her phone rang, its shrill tone jarring against the peaceful atmosphere she'd been trying to cultivate. Frowning, she wiped her hands on a dish towel and checked the screen.

"Deputy Director Irvin?" she muttered, puzzled by the unexpected call. It had been ages since she'd last spoken to him. Hesitantly, she swiped to answer. "Sir?"

"Agent Cross," Irvin's voice was warm and fatherly, like she remembered it. It had been a while since they'd spoke. Irvin was the one who'd made Morgan an agent again after her time in prison. "It's good to hear your voice," he said. "I've heard about the solid work you've been doing recently. You're making us proud."

"Thank you, sir," she replied, taken aback by the praise. "But if you don't mind me asking, why are you calling? I'm on vacation."

"Ah, yes. Your well-deserved time off." He chuckled softly, and Morgan couldn't help but feel a prickle of unease. "I apologize for disturbing you, but there's a matter I'd like to discuss."

Morgan's grip on the phone tightened, her knuckles turning white. She glanced at Skunk, who seemed to have caught on to her tension and was now watching her with concern. "What kind of matter, sir?"

"Something I believe you'll want to hear about," he said cryptically.

Morgan's heart raced as she anticipated Irvin's response, the tension in her shoulders making it difficult to maintain a casual stance. Skunk whined softly, pawing at her leg as if trying to offer comfort. She scratched his head absentmindedly, her focus on the phone call.

"Agent Cross," Irvin began, his voice grave. "I know you're on vacation, but I'm afraid we could use your help. Mueller is temporarily off, and I've taken over in Dallas. Something's come up that requires your attention."

The words hung heavy in the air, and Morgan felt her stomach tighten. Surely, they would have waited until she returned from vacation if it wasn't something important. She gritted her teeth, frustration bubbling beneath the surface.

"Sir, with all due respect, I earned this time off. Can't someone else handle it?" Her voice was firm but respectful – she didn't want to appear ungrateful for the break, but she couldn't help feeling cheated out of her hard-earned rest.

Irvin sighed on the other end of the line, the sound filling Morgan's ear like a gust of wind. "I understand your concerns, Cross, but our resources are stretched thin, and your expertise is needed. I wouldn't ask this of you if it wasn't absolutely necessary."

Morgan closed her eyes, her jaw clenched as she fought the urge to argue further. She knew that people depended on her, both within the FBI and those affected by the cases she worked on. Her sense of duty warred with her need for respite, an internal battle raging within her.

"Fine," she finally conceded, exhaling sharply. "What's going on?"

"There's a new killer targeting women in Dallas, and Derik Greene is working the case. He needs his partner."

Morgan's grip tightened on the phone as she processed the information. Her heart raced with a mix of anger and fear, the thought of another killer on the loose sending shivers down her spine. She glanced at Skunk, who had picked up on her anxiety and was now watching her intently from the doorway.

"Derik can handle himself," she muttered, her voice tight with frustration. "He doesn't need me there holding his hand."

"Of course not," Irvin agreed, though the concern in his voice betrayed his true thoughts. "But it's always better when the two of you work together. You both have unique skills that complement each other, and we need that expertise now more than ever. If you can't make it, I understand. But I'm worried about this killer, Morgan. We all are."

The weight of responsibility settled heavily on her shoulders. She knew that turning away wouldn't change the fact that lives were at risk, and the thought of doing nothing while innocent people suffered made her sick to her stomach. Forcing herself to take a deep breath, Morgan steeled her resolve.

"Thank you for the offer, sir," she said, her voice firm. "I'll consider it and let you know."

"Take your time, Morgan," Irvin replied, understanding in his tone. "Just remember that every second counts."

The call ended with a click, leaving Morgan alone with her thoughts and the ghostly whispers of the wind. As she stood there, torn between duty and self-preservation, the memories of her father's cabin seemed to press in around her, both comforting and suffocating all at once.

Of course, she couldn't just ignore a case, not when lives were at stake. But leaving the comfort and safety of her father's cabin felt like abandoning a piece of herself, a chance to uncover long-buried secrets and heal old wounds.

"Come on, Skunk," she called out to her loyal Pitbull, who was sniffing around the yard. "We need to go."

With a whine, Skunk trotted over, his tail drooping in disappointment. Morgan ruffled his fur affectionately before heading back inside to pack their belongings.

***

The car tore through the forest, kicking up dust and gravel as it sped down the winding path. Skunk sat in the passenger seat next to Morgan, his head hanging low as he whined softly. He could sense her turmoil, the inner battle between duty and personal desire that was tearing her apart.

"Hey, buddy," Morgan said soothingly, reaching over to scratch him behind the ears. "I know, I wish we didn't have to leave so soon either. But we'll come back, I promise."

Skunk licked her hand in response, his eyes filled with concern and understanding. Morgan smiled sadly as she continued to drive, her grip on the steering wheel tight as she tried to steady her racing thoughts.

Her father's face swam in her mind, his smile warm, and his eyes filled with love. The cabin held so many memories, so much laughter and joy, but also an undercurrent of sadness, of things left unsaid and secrets still buried deep. And yet, despite everything, she knew she had to put those feelings aside for now – there were people counting on her, and she couldn't let them down.

"Sometimes, Skunk," she continued, her voice soft and weary, "I wonder if I'm really cut out for this job. If maybe I'm just chasing after something I can never truly have."

Skunk whined again, nuzzling his head against her arm in silent sympathy. Morgan smiled, grateful for the support and love of her faithful companion. At least she could always trust her dog.

The forest began to thin as Morgan sped down the winding road, her grip on the steering wheel tight. Skunk, sensing her tension, let out a soft whine from the passenger seat.

In the rearview mirror, the dense trees grew smaller and smaller until they were nothing but a faint blur. Although she hadn't seen anyone near the cabin, a nagging feeling clung to her like a stubborn shadow – the sensation that they hadn't truly been alone.

Damn FBI. It was infuriating how they could just swoop in and disrupt her plans, yanking her away from the solitude she craved. Yet, deep down, she couldn't deny the relief that washed over her as well. The cabin, with its ghosts of the past and memories that clawed at her heart, had become an almost unbearable weight.

Morgan took a deep breath, trying to push aside the conflicting emotions churning within her. She had a job to do, people who needed her help. And maybe, just maybe, throwing herself into work was exactly what she needed to keep the shadows of the past at bay.

Morgan's knuckles turned white as she clenched the steering wheel, her eyes focused on the road, but her mind was elsewhere. A vivid memory of her father surfaced, unbidden - the two of them sitting on the porch of the cabin, fishing rods in hand, laughter filling the air as they reeled in their catch.

"Always be patient, Morgan," her father had said, his voice echoing in her mind like a ghostly whisper. *"The best things in life are worth waiting for."*

How could he have hid something so major from her? If he really was in the FBI... how could he not tell her? Morgan wondered if she had the right to feel betrayed. Her father was dead now. There were no apologies to be had, no conversations of reconciliation.

A sudden jolt of panic shot through her as she realized she'd been lost in the memory, her focus drifting dangerously from the road. She jerked back to attention just in time to swerve around a curve, narrowly avoiding a collision with the guardrail.

"Damn it!" she cursed under her breath, her heart pounding wildly in her chest. She could feel the sweat forming at her temples, the lingering fear from the near-accident sending tremors down her spine.

"Sorry, Skunk," she murmured, reaching over to give the dog a reassuring pat. "I promise I'll get you home safe, buddy. Just need to clear my head first."

But even as she tried to refocus on the task at hand, she couldn't shake the feeling that her father's memory was trying to tell her something, guiding her from beyond the grave.

CHAPTER THREE

An hour later, Morgan pulled up at the crime scene, still reeling from her close call on the road. The flashing red and blue lights of the police cars cast lights across the face of the building where they had congregated, the stark contrast of light and darkness reflecting the turmoil inside her. It was getting late, and the sun had already long set.

"Alright, Skunk," she said as she turned off the engine, her voice wavering with exhaustion. "You stay here for now, okay? I'll come back and take you home as soon as I can."

Skunk whined in response as Morgan left him in the car. She had come straight here after talking to Irvin on the phone and getting more details, and he made it sound a lot more urgent than he had earlier.

The crime scene was a frenzy of activity, agents and officers moving with a sense of urgency that only came with fresh leads and a killer on the loose. Morgan took a steadying breath, pushing aside her personal struggles as she stepped into the fray, determined to bring justice to those who needed it most.

She spotted Derik, his dark hair slicked back, hands in the pockets of his slacks. Morgan jogged over to him, her heart pounding not just from exertion but also from the awkwardness of seeing him again. She had told him to focus on his son, and yet here he was, still entrenched in the case. His presence was a reminder of betrayal, and Morgan knew she needed time before she could trust him again. Maybe she never would.

"Hey," she muttered, her voice barely audible above the distant hum of traffic.

"Hey," Derik replied, his sharp green eyes avoiding hers, his face paler and gaunt with slight stubble growing in. "You're here... I'm glad. You should see this."

He led her through the crime scene tape and into the dark alley, where the sinister glow of emergency lights illuminated the young woman's lifeless form. She couldn't have been much older than twenty, sprawled on the cold, unforgiving pavement, her dressing robe draped around her like a shroud. The delicate lace gloves that adorned her hands, which were seemingly glued together, seemed incongruous against the brutality of her fate.

"Beauty pageant contestant?" Morgan asked, unable to suppress a shudder as she took in the tragic scene.

"Elizabeth 'Lizzie' Meadows," Derik confirmed, his voice tight with anger. "Seems like she was taken right out of her dressing room. Disappeared last night. Nobody knew where she was, until we got a call that someone had found her in this alleyway... that was only a couple hours ago, but we presume she died last night."

Morgan tried to make sense of the senseless. What kind of monster would abduct a vulnerable young woman, only to discard her so callously in an alley? And what did the gloves signify, some twisted trophy for the killer?

"Any leads on a suspect?" Morgan asked, forcing herself to focus on the task at hand.

Derik shook his head, frustration etched across his features. "Nothing solid yet, but we're working on it."

"Good," Morgan replied, her voice steely with determination. "We need to make sure whoever did this pays for it."

With a deep breath, Morgan crouched down next to the lifeless form of Lizzie Meadows. Her eyes traced over the body, searching for any clues that might lead them closer to the killer. The dressing robe pooled around her on the grimy pavement, and Morgan couldn't help but think of how out of place its soft fabric seemed in such a harsh environment.

"Her gloves," Morgan murmured, more to herself than to Derik. She reached out with gloved fingers and gingerly prodded the lace that encased Lizzie's hands. Her eyebrows furrowed as she felt something odd beneath the delicate material. "They're glued to her hands."

"It appears that way," Derik said. "I doubt she did it herself."

Morgan shook her head, frustration coursing through her. They were dealing with a twisted individual, that much was clear. But what was the significance of the glued gloves? Were they meant to be some sort of message?

"Wait until you hear this," Derik said, attempting to catch Morgan's attention. "The strangest part is that there's no sign she struggled or fought back. It's like she just... collapsed here. We can't see a cause of death, at least not yet."

Morgan's brow creased further as she processed this new piece of information. Every instinct she had screamed that something was off about this whole situation. But what could cause a perfectly healthy young woman to drop dead without a struggle? And how did the killer manage to glue the gloves onto her hands without leaving a trace?

As she mulled over these questions, Morgan felt an unsettling sensation creep up her spine - the nagging feeling that she was missing something crucial. She glanced at Derik, who seemed just as lost as she was, before focusing back on Lizzie's body.

"Let's get forensics in here to finish this up," she told Derik.

***

The shadows cast by the towering buildings on either side of the alley seemed to reach out, clawing at the small group of investigators who stood huddled together, their breath misting in the cold air. Morgan leaned against the wall, arms folded across her chest as she watched forensics comb through the scene. The muted hum of activity was punctuated by the occasional snap of a camera shutter and the quiet murmur of voices.

"Derik," she said, turning to her partner. "What makes the FBI think this is the work of a killer?"

"Based on witness accounts, someone saw Lizzie with a man just before she died," Derik replied, his voice low and serious. "We haven't been able to locate him yet, but the circumstances surrounding her death are... strange, to say the least."

Morgan nodded, recalling the glued gloves and the lack of struggle. A shiver ran down her spine, though she wasn't sure if it was from the chill in the air or the unsettling nature of the case. "No visible wounds, no signs of a struggle... It's like the killer just willed her to drop dead."

"Exactly," Derik agreed, rubbing his hands together for warmth. "It's baffling."

In her mind's eye, she pictured Lizzie collapsing to the ground, her life slipping away without so much as a whimper – and it made her sick to her stomach. Who could do such a thing? And why?

"Whatever happened here," Morgan muttered, more to herself than to Derik, "we need to find that man and bring him to justice. No one should be able to kill so effortlessly and walk away without a trace."

"Agreed," Derik nodded. "We'll find him, Morgan. You can count on that."

19

Morgan's gaze flicked to the bustling forensic team one last time before turning to Derik. "Call me when the coroner's report comes in. I've had too many long drives lately, and Skunk needs to get home."

"Will do, Morgan," Derik said with a nod, his eyes betraying the unease they both felt about this case.

Morgan started walking back to her car, her footsteps echoing through the dim alley. She couldn't shake the feeling of dread that settled in her chest, like icy tendrils wrapping around her heart. This case was different, and she knew it deep in her bones.

"Special Agent Morgan Cross?"

The unfamiliar voice made her pause, and she turned to see a tall, lean man approaching her. His hair was a short and dark blond, but tousled in a way, and his wide blue eyes held an expression of awe that seemed out of place in the grim alleyway. But he was wearing an FBI jacket, so he was obviously one of theirs.

"Can I help you?" Morgan asked, studying him cautiously. He must have been a couple years younger than her--maybe thirty-seven or thirty-eight.

"Uh, yes," he stammered, extending a hand. "I'm Agent Thomas Grady. I specialize in cyber security and software… I just wanted to introduce myself."

"Nice to meet you, Thomas." Morgan shook his hand firmly, noting the firmness of his grip. "Welcome to the team."

"Thank you, Special Agent Cross." Thomas's eyes brightened, and he let out a small, nervous laugh. "I've heard so much about your work. You're something of a legend around here."

Morgan offered a tight smile in response. The weight of her past accomplishments – and the shadows that still haunted her – lay heavy on her shoulders. "Well, I just try to do my job and catch the bad guys. It's what we all signed up for, right?"

"Absolutely," Thomas agreed enthusiastically, though his voice wavered as he glanced back at the crime scene. "It's just… I never thought I'd be working on a case like this."

"None of us ever do," Morgan replied, her voice softening. She knew that the reality of working in the field could be a harsh awakening for new agents. "Listen, Thomas, it's not always going to be easy, but we're all here to support each other. If you ever need anything, don't hesitate to ask."

"Thank you, Special Agent Cross," he said, his gratitude evident in his eyes.

"Call me Morgan," she told him with a slight nod.

Morgan's eyes flicked over to Derik, who was standing a short distance away. His face was tight as he watched her and Thomas converse, his eyes narrowing with what seemed like suspicion--or maybe even jealousy. Morgan wasn't sure what to do with that information, so she ignored it.

"Excuse me," Morgan said politely to Thomas, nodding towards her car. "I have to be somewhere."

"Of course," Thomas replied, stepping back. "It was nice meeting you, Morgan."

"Good luck out here," she said, offering a small smile before heading toward her car. It was late to be starting a case, and until she had more to work with, she needed to get her dog home.

CHAPTER FOUR

For the rest of the night, Derik didn't call. Morgan fell into an uneasy sleep. Her dreams were filled with haunting images of her past life – the prison cell that had housed her for ten years, the bloodied hands of the faceless men who had framed her for murder, and feeling of betrayal.

Morgan's heart raced, her body slick with sweat, as she tried in vain to escape the ghosts of her past. The feeling of helplessness and despair threatened to overwhelm her, but no matter how hard she fought, she couldn't break free from the darkness that enveloped her.

She awoke with a start, gasping for air as she clutched the sheets that tangled around her legs. Her heart pounded in her chest, and she could still feel the phantom weight of the prison bars pressing down on her.

"Damn it," Morgan whispered harshly, running a hand through her damp hair. Another restless night. She knew she wouldn't find any comfort in trying to sleep again – not tonight.

With a heavy heart, Morgan decided that sleep was a luxury she couldn't afford tonight. She swung her legs over the edge of the bed and stood up, feeling the cold hardwood floor beneath her feet. Skunk lifted his head from his own bed in the corner of the room, his ears perked up as he watched her intently.

"Let's go," she whispered to him, her voice barely audible. The loyal dog followed her into the living room, where moonlight seeped through the curtains, casting long shadows across the floor.

Morgan poured herself a glass of scotch and settled down on the couch, case files spread out before her like a dark puzzle waiting to be solved. Skunk lay down beside her, resting his chin on his paws, his eyes never leaving her face.

"Something isn't right about these gloves," she muttered under her breath, sipping her drink. Her fingers traced the outline of Lizzie Meadows's photo, the young beauty queen staring back at her with a smile that hid a thousand secrets.

Who were you, Lizzie? Morgan wondered, searching for answers in the dead girl's eyes. *Why did someone want you dead?*

As she delved deeper into Lizzie's life, she found a world of cutthroat competition and ruthless ambition. Pageants had been her entire existence, a stage upon which she danced for adoring crowds and judgmental eyes. Her parents had pushed her relentlessly, molding her into their vision of perfection.

It was sickening. Those pageants – they exploited children, robbed them of their innocence. And for what? A shiny crown and a few minutes of fame? Morgan couldn't understand it.

Skunk whined softly as if in agreement, nuzzling her hand with his wet nose. Morgan spared him a brief smile before turning her attention back to the case.

The glow of the computer screen cast eerie shadows across Morgan's face as she continued her search through the darkest corners of Lizzie Meadows's past. She decided to check Lizzie's record, just in case.

Lizzie only had one thing on her record, a case that had been dropped because it had happened before she'd turned eighteen, but only briefly went to trial after. As she read the details, a horrifying story unfolded.

Abigail Jones – a shy, quiet girl who had once been friends with Lizzie – ended her life in their senior year of high school. A torrent of cruel messages and public humiliation led the girl to believe she had no way out.

And at the center of it all was none other than Lizzie Meadows.

"Jesus Christ," Morgan whispered, feeling a wave of fury rise within her. She knew people could be cruel, but this was beyond anything she'd imagined.

Her hand tightened around the glass of whiskey clenched in her fist, the amber liquid sloshing dangerously close to the rim. It took every ounce of restraint not to hurl the glass against the wall in anger.

Morgan's mind raced with thoughts, trying to make sense of Lizzie's actions and how they might connect to her murder. Was it possible that someone had sought revenge for Abigail's death? Or was there something more sinister at play?

Nothing was ever that simple, was it? Her gaze once again drawn to the haunting photos of Lizzie Meadows. A beautiful young woman with a deadly secret hidden behind her dazzling smile.

Morgan's fingers flew across the keyboard, her brow furrowed with determination. It seemed as though Lizzie's harassment of Abigail Jones had been effectively wiped from the internet – no news articles, no social media posts, nothing. The only trace she could find was a single thread on an obscure forum where users debated the legitimacy of the allegations.

"Someone went to great lengths to bury this," Morgan muttered under her breath, Skunk curled up at her feet. She scrolled through the forum, noting the conflicting opinions and heated arguments. One user claimed to have inside knowledge of the situation, but their account had since been deleted.

As if on cue, her phone began to vibrate on the table beside her. The screen displayed 5:00 AM, and Morgan felt a sinking sensation in her stomach. She knew that early morning calls were rarely good news.

"Cross," she answered tersely, her grip tightening on the phone.

"Morgan, it's Derik." His voice sounded strained, and Morgan could sense the urgency in his tone. "We've got another victim."

CHAPTER FIVE

The tires of Morgan's car screeched against the damp pavement as she pulled up outside the concert hall, where the most recent victim had allegedly been found. The dim streetlights cast an eerie glow over the building, shrouding it in shadows and giving it a sinister appearance. She stepped out into the morning air, her breath visible as she exhaled.

"Over here," Derik called out from near the entrance. He stood with his hands shoved deep into his pockets, his face tense. "Janitor found the body inside."

"Another one with the gloves?" Morgan asked, her voice taut with anger and frustration.

"Seems like it," he replied grimly. "Let's go."

As they entered the darkened concert hall, Morgan's heart pounded heavily in her chest. The faint smell of stale perfume and sweat hung in the air, a remnant of the previous evening's performances. Her jaw tightened, knowing that the horror that awaited them was far removed from the world of music and celebration.

In the center of the stage, illuminated by a single spotlight, was the body. A young woman lay face-down on the keys of a grand piano. Her hair cascaded around her head like a macabre halo, and her feet dangled limply off the edge of the stage. The way she was positioned made it seem like she was merely part of a twisted performance.

"Jesus," Morgan whispered, her stomach twisting in knots. White silky gloves encased the woman's hands, glued to her skin with an almost surgical precision. It was a chilling echo of Lizzie Meadows's death, and Morgan knew there had to be a connection.

"Same MO as before," Derik confirmed, his voice hushed. "Gloves glued to the hands, no obvious cause of death."

"Any connections between the victims yet?" Morgan asked, her mind racing with possibilities. She remembered the hidden truths she'd uncovered about Lizzie's past – could there be a similar secret lurking behind this woman's life?

"Still working on it," he replied, his gaze never leaving the gruesome scene before them.

"Find out everything you can about her," Morgan instructed, her voice firm. "Friends, family, enemies… anything that could lead us to who did this."

"Of course," Derik nodded.

Morgan crouched beside the lifeless body, her heart pounding in her chest. She felt a mixture of anger and dread gnawing at her insides, fueled by the sight of those haunting white gloves glued to the victim's hands.

"Excuse me! I know this woman!" a voice called out, cutting through the tension in the room. Morgan glanced up to see a man in his fifties, dressed in an impeccably tailored suit, followed closely by a pair of uniformed officers. "I'm Roger Walter, chairman of this concert hall."

"Mr. Walter," Morgan acknowledged tersely, not taking her eyes off the body. "You say you know this woman?"

"Yes," he replied, his face pale but composed. "Her name is Amy Sanderson. She was here for a limited engagement, performing several concerts." He hesitated for a moment, swallowing hard before continuing. "She was incredibly talented… it's such a tragedy."

"Did you notice anything unusual or suspicious lately?" Morgan asked, studying Roger's face for any sign of deceit.

"Nothing that comes to mind," he said, shaking his head. "She seemed… happy, focused on her performances."

Morgan frowned, her instincts telling her that there was more to the story than what Roger was revealing. She cataloged his reaction in her mind, another piece of the puzzle to explore later.

"Mr. Walter," Morgan said, her eyes narrowing as she regarded the chairman. "I need a list of names. Everyone who was in this concert hall last night. We'll need to talk to them all."

Roger's expression shifted from composed to mildly agitated, his gaze darting around the room for a moment before settling back on Morgan. "Agent Cross, that might be… difficult."

"Difficult?" Morgan echoed, disbelief creeping into her tone. "Why?"

"Because there were two large concerts held here last night," Roger explained, gesturing with a sweep of his hand towards the grand stage. "The halls were fully booked, filled with attendees, staff, and performers. It could have been anyone."

Morgan clenched her fists, frustration simmering beneath the surface. She knew that time was of the essence in cases like these, and every obstacle only increased the chances of the killer slipping through their fingers.

"Fine," she bit out, her voice sharp and controlled. "Then we start with the obvious. The performers, the staff members working last night, the people who had keys or access codes to restricted areas. We'll work our way out from there."

"Very well," Roger acquiesced, though Morgan could tell he wasn't thrilled about the prospect. "I'll have my staff compile the information you requested."

"Good," Morgan replied, her gaze drifting back to Amy's lifeless form on the piano. "Roger, when was the last time you saw Amy?" Morgan asked, her eyes flicking from the body to the concert hall chairman.

"Ah, well... I believe it was the day before yesterday," Roger hesitated, wiping his sweaty palms on his pants. "She preferred to rehearse in total isolation, so I didn't see her at all yesterday before her show."

Morgan raised an eyebrow, taking note of the slight tremor in his voice. She filed away the information, knowing that even the smallest detail could prove crucial later on. Despite her frustration with Roger's lack of knowledge, she couldn't help but empathize with the man. They were all on edge, and he was no exception.

"Alright, thank you," Morgan said curtly, her gaze scanning the room for any other potential leads.

That was when she spotted him – a figure lingering in the shadows by the stage door, observing the proceedings with keen interest. He wore a gray jumpsuit.

The janitor.

He must have been the one to find the body.

"Get that list to us now," she told Roger, not waiting for a reply before striding towards the janitor.

Maybe he knew more than he had been letting on.

CHAPTER SIX

"Can I have a word with you?" Morgan asked the janitor, her tone firm yet respectful. The janitor nodded, his eyes darting nervously between Morgan and the crime scene. He was a gaunt-faced man, tall and thin, with gray stubble lining his chin.

"Oh--of course," he replied shakily, swallowing hard as if trying to keep his composure. "What can I do for you? I already told the police everything I know, and I talked to that other guy... the agent."

"That would be my partner, Special Agent Derik Greene," Morgan said. She flashed her FBI badge. "My name is Special Agent Morgan Cross. Tell me about the night of the concerts," Morgan began, her mind racing with questions. "Did you notice anything unusual or out of place? Did you see anyone you didn't recognize or anyone acting suspicious?"

"Well... I don't know."

The janitor's eyes flicked over Morgan's shoulder in the direction where she'd just been talking to Roger. Morgan looked back to see Roger was gone--hopefully, compiling that damn list she'd asked for.

"Over here," the janitor said.

As they moved into the seclusion of the dimly lit corner, Morgan studied the lines etched into the janitor's face — a roadmap of years spent cleaning up after others and keeping this place running smoothly. She felt a pang of sympathy for him; finding a body like this was likely something he'd never forget.

"Can you tell me about when you found the body?" she asked.

"Uh, yeah. I was doin' my usual rounds, cleanin' up after last night's concerts," he began, his voice wavering slightly. "I came in here to sweep the stage and... there she was. Just lyin' there on the piano, like some kinda twisted art piece."

Morgan could hear the tremor in his voice and see the haunted look in his eyes. He had been going about his day, just trying to do his job, and then he'd stumbled upon a grisly scene that would be forever etched into his memory.

"Thank you for sharing that," she said softly, her empathy shining through. "I know it must be difficult."

"Yeah, well," he muttered, rubbing the back of his neck. "It ain't somethin' you expect to see, that's for sure."

Morgan nodded, her mind racing with questions and possibilities. This case was proving to be more complex than she'd anticipated, and she couldn't afford to miss any crucial details.

"Is there anything else you think I should know?" she asked, her gaze never leaving his face. "Anything that might help us figure out what happened to Ms. Sanderson?"

The janitor hesitated for a moment, his eyes darting around the room as if searching for an answer.

The janitor looked down at his hands for a moment before meeting her gaze again. "Well, now that you mention it," he began hesitantly, "I did hear something else. I was passing by Ms. Sanderson's rehearsal studio when I heard raised voices – an argument."

"An argument?" Morgan's interest was piqued. "Could you tell who was involved?"

"Pretty sure one of 'em was Roger – Mr. Walter, that is. The chairman." He paused, scratching his head. "The other voice must've been Ms. Sanderson's. I couldn't make out what they were saying, but it sounded pretty heated."

Morgan's brow furrowed as suspicion bloomed within her. According to what Roger had told her earlier, he hadn't seen Amy since the day before yesterday. But here was the janitor, claiming to have heard them arguing just last night. Something wasn't adding up.

"Thank you," she said gravely. "That's very helpful."

"Sure thing, Agent Cross," the janitor replied, relief evident in his expression. "Just tryin' to do my part."

As Morgan walked away from the janitor, her mind raced. If Roger was lying about his interaction with the victim, what else might he be hiding? For now, he was her prime suspect, and she needed to dig deeper to uncover the truth.

She replayed the events of the day in her head, searching for any inconsistencies or clues she might have missed. The image of Amy's lifeless body, her hands encased in those pristine white gloves, haunted her thoughts. What twisted mind could have orchestrated such a horrific scene?

Morgan clenched her fists, determination settling over her like a cloak. She needed to find Roger, and he couldn't have gotten far.

Just as Morgan was about to head into the hallway, her phone buzzed. She took it out, only to see the coroner's name. She answered it and said, "This is Cross."

"Special Agent Cross," the coroner said, "we need to talk."

CHAPTER SEVEN

Morgan Cross stood just outside the concert hall, phone pressed to her ear, attention drawn away from the chaos of uniformed officers and crime scene investigators buzzing around the grand piano. The humid, early morning air bit at her cheeks, but she barely noticed it as she listened to the voice on the other end of the line. It was the coroner, Steve McCabe, his words sending a shiver down her spine.

"Poison," Steve said, sounding almost as surprised as Morgan felt. "The cause of death for Lizzie Meadows wasn't blunt force trauma or strangulation. It was poison."

"Poison?" Morgan repeated, her brow furrowing. Her mind raced, trying to make sense of this new piece of information. "What kind of poison?"

"Still working on identifying it," Steve replied. "But it seems to have entered her bloodstream through her hands. Some sort of a powder, maybe, although I can't say for sure yet. We're running a chemical analysis on the gloves the victim was wearing on her hands."

"Poison?" Morgan asked, her voice barely above a whisper. "What kind of poison are we talking about here, Steve?"

"Something potent," Steve replied on the other end of the line. "A rare and fast-acting compound that targeted the nervous system."

Morgan's mind raced as she tried to make sense of this new information. The killer had gone through the trouble of gluing the victim's hands together, only to poison them. It seemed like a bizarre method, but she knew better than to underestimate the twisted minds of criminals.

"Steve," she pressed, "how did the poison enter her bloodstream? Was it ingested or injected?"

"Neither," he replied, his voice tense with concern. "It appears the poison was some form of powder that was used beneath the gloves and glue. The substance seeped into the victim's skin, eventually making its way into her bloodstream."

Morgan's heart pounded in her chest as the full gravity of the situation sank in. If the killer had used the same method with Amy Sanderson, they needed to act quickly to prevent further harm.

"Steve, we have a new victim here," Morgan said urgently. "I need you to run the same tests on her ASAP. We're sending her down to the morgue now."

"Understood," Steve replied, his voice heavy with the weight of the task at hand. "I'll be ready for her when she arrives."

"Thanks, Steve." With a click, Morgan ended the call and quickly turned her attention to finding Roger Walter.

Morgan's footsteps echoed through the empty backstage halls as she navigated the labyrinthine passageways of the concert hall. Her jaw clenched in frustration, she couldn't shake the feeling that something was amiss with Roger Walter. The lies, the evasiveness… it all added up to someone with something to hide.

She stormed back into the main hall, where the body was, along with most of the personnel, including Derik, who was directing the crime scene investigators.

Morgan stormed right up to Derik. "Where's Roger Walter?"

"Left," Derik replied, nonchalantly. "Said he had some business to take care of. His secretary is printing the list you asked for."

"Dammit, Greene!" Morgan snapped, her controlled demeanor slipping for a moment. "How could you let him leave? We're not done with him!"

"Chill, Cross," Derik defended himself, holding up his hands. "He'd already given us everything we needed. Besides, he asked to go, and I didn't see any reason to hold him back."

"Every reason!" she fumed, clenching her fists. But she knew better than to waste time arguing with Derik right now. Time was of the essence.

Without another word, Morgan stormed off in search of the elusive Roger Walter. Her footsteps echoed on the polished marble floors of the concert hall, her heels clicking like a metronome counting down the seconds. The lingering scent of expensive perfume mingled with the faintest whiff of decay, a stark reminder of the twisted horrors hidden beneath the elegant façade.

Her gaze narrowed as she spotted the front desk, where a prim secretary sat, typing away at her computer. Morgan approached her, her voice sharp and insistent. "I'm Special Agent Cross with the FBI. I need to know where Roger Walter went. Now."

The secretary looked up, startled by Morgan's intensity. She hesitated, glancing around nervously before answering. "Uh, I think he left for the day. Said something about Fort Worth…"

"Damn it," Morgan muttered, her heart pounding in her chest. Roger was slipping through their fingers, and she couldn't shake the feeling that they were missing something crucial. She needed to find him – fast.

"Listen," Morgan continued, leaning in closer to the secretary and locking eyes with her. "I need you to tell me everything you know about Roger Walter's whereabouts. Every detail matters."

The secretary swallowed hard, intimidated by Morgan's unwavering gaze. She knew better than to withhold information from the FBI. And so, she began to divulge what little she knew, hoping it would be enough to help Agent Cross find the elusive chairman.

"Where exactly did Roger go? I need specifics," Morgan demanded, her murky green eyes boring into the secretary's.

"Uh, he mentioned a concert hall in Fort Worth," the secretary stammered, hastily checking her notes. "He left about ten minutes ago. Said he'd be back in a few days."

"Ten minutes?" Morgan clenched her fists, her nails biting into her palms. She could feel her anger boiling just below the surface, threatening to spill over. She took a deep breath, trying to regain control. She had let him slip away, and now she was playing catch-up. Was it too late?

"Did he say where he was going before Fort Worth?" she pressed, her voice taut with urgency.

"Home, I think," the secretary replied, her voice barely above a whisper. "To pack some things."

Morgan's eyes darted to the clock on the wall. Ten minutes – ten minutes was all that separated her from Roger Walter. She couldn't let him get away, not when he held vital information to this case.

"Give me his address," Morgan demanded, blood pounding in her ears as adrenaline coursed through her veins.

The secretary hesitated for a moment before complying, quickly scribbling down an address on a slip of paper. Morgan snatched it from her fingers, her mind working in overdrive as she strategized her next move. She needed to act fast.

"Thank you," she muttered, already turning on her heel and striding towards the exit. Each step felt like a race against time, as if the fate of the investigation hung in the balance.

"Hey, Morgan!" Derik called out, jogging over to her with a look of concern etched across his face. "What's going on? You look like you're about to jump out of your skin."

"Roger got away," she spat, frustration simmering beneath her words. "He left ten minutes ago, and I have a sinking feeling that if we don't catch up to him, we'll never find out the truth."

"I don't understand, Cross, why is he a suspect now?"

"He lied about the last time he saw Amy, Derik," Morgan said. "The janitor heard them arguing yesterday, but Roger said he hadn't seen her since the day before."

Derik's eyes widened, and he nodded in understanding. "What can I do?"

"Send a team to his house," Morgan instructed, her voice firm and unwavering. "I'm going after him myself. We need to cover all our bases."

"Got it," Derik said, his tone equally resolute. "Be careful, Morgan."

Morgan's heart pounded in her chest as she pushed through the concert hall doors, leaving Derik behind. The urgency to find Roger Walter fueled her every step. Her breath came out in short, rapid bursts as she jogged towards her car.

She couldn't afford to waste a moment. This was her chance to pull back the veil of deception and expose the truth, not just for herself, but for all those affected by this heinous criminal. The lives of innocent people were at stake, and she would not let them down.

"Damn it," Morgan muttered under her breath as she fumbled with her keys, trying to unlock her car door. "Get it together."

Finally, she managed to get the door open and slid into the driver's seat. In seconds, the engine roared to life, and she sped off into the street.

CHAPTER EIGHT

The heavy bags of groceries threatened to topple Lisa over as she struggled up the walkway to her front door. The paper handles dug painfully into her fingers, and she cursed under her breath.

Her arms felt like they were on fire, the weight of the groceries straining her muscles to their limit. But she couldn't stop now; she was so close to the safety of her home.

"Almost there," she whispered, gritting her teeth and taking another step. "Just a little further."

As she finally reached the front door, a bead of sweat trickled down her forehead, and she blinked it away. She knew that once she was inside, she could set the bags down and take a much-needed break. But first, she had to navigate the seemingly insurmountable task of unlocking the door without dropping her precious cargo.

With a deep breath, she steadied herself and carefully inserted the key into the lock. Just a few more agonizing seconds, and she'd be home free.

Just as Lisa was about to turn the key, a figure jogged into view from her peripheral vision. She startled slightly, her heart skipping a beat as she glanced over at the newcomer.

"Hey there!" the man called out, slowing to a stop beside her. "You look like you could use some help with those bags."

Lisa blinked, taking in the stranger's friendly smile and disheveled brown hair. There was something vaguely familiar about him, but she couldn't quite put her finger on it. He looked harmless enough, but she hesitated for a moment, her instincts warring with her desire for assistance.

"Um, sure," she finally said, her voice uncertain. "Thank you."

"No problem," the man replied cheerfully, reaching out to take the heaviest bag from her grasp. Lisa felt a wave of relief wash over her as the strain on her arm lessened, and she offered him a grateful smile.

"Really, I appreciate it," she told him, unlocking the door and pushing it open. "I didn't think these bags would be so heavy when I picked them up at the store."

The man laughed, his eyes crinkling at the corners. "Yeah, I've been there before. It's always a surprise how much groceries can weigh."

As they stepped inside the foyer, Lisa couldn't shake the nagging feeling that she knew this man from somewhere. She studied his face as he set the grocery bag on the floor next to hers, trying to place him.

"Have we met before?" she asked, curiosity getting the better of her.

"Maybe," he said, evasively. "I feel like I've seen you around town."

"Could be," Lisa muttered, still puzzling over his identity. She brushed the thought aside for now, deciding it wasn't important. What mattered was that this kind stranger had helped her carry her groceries inside, and she owed him her thanks.

"Anyways," she said, forcing a smile. "I really appreciate the help. So, thank you."

"Of course," he replied, his eyes meeting hers for a brief moment before glancing away. "It was my pleasure."

"Alright then," Lisa said, feeling slightly awkward now that the task at hand was completed. "Well, have a good day."

"Hey, um, do you mind if I ask for a glass of water?" the man said suddenly, his voice strained. "I've been walking all morning and could really use some."

Lisa hesitated, feeling a tinge of discomfort surge through her. Was it safe to let this stranger linger in her home? She shook off her paranoia, chiding herself for being overly suspicious. The man had helped her, after all; getting him a glass of water was the least she could do.

"Sure," Lisa said, forcing another smile. "Just give me a moment."

As she filled a glass at the kitchen sink, she couldn't help but steal glances at the man by the front door. He stood there, shifting his weight from one foot to the other, looking almost as uneasy as she felt. A part of her wondered if he sensed her apprehension, but she dismissed the thought as soon as it entered her mind.

"Here you go," Lisa said, handing him the glass of water. Her hand brushed against his as she did so, and for a split second, she felt an unsettling chill race up her spine. The man's eyes locked onto hers, and she quickly looked away, her heart pounding in her chest.

"Thank you," he muttered, taking a long sip of water.

Lisa's gaze lingered on the man's hands as he drank from the glass. It was odd--he was wearing... gloves. Black gloves, even though it was a warm morning, and he said he'd been walking a lot.

And something about those gloves were... familiar.

A memory flickered in Lisa's mind, and her eyes widened as she remembered where she'd seen this man and his gloves before.

But it was too late. The man lunged forward, slamming the glass of water onto the floor and sending shards flying. His hand shot out, gripping her throat with a vice-like strength that left her gasping for air. Panic bubbled up inside her, clawing at her chest like a wild animal.

"Help!" Lisa choked out, desperately trying to pry his fingers from her throat. But her vision blurred, dark spots dancing before her eyes as her body began to betray her.

"Nobody can help you now," the man whispered, his voice cold and devoid of emotion. He tightened his grip, and Lisa knew that her time was running out.

CHAPTER NINE

Morgan pulled up to Roger Walter's house, her FBI badge hanging from a lanyard around her neck. She glanced at the driveway and saw his car parked there, confirming that he hadn't slipped away yet. A wave of determination washed over her; she couldn't let him escape justice.

Stay focused, Morgan, she told herself, stepping out of her car and walking up the path to the front door. *You've got this.*

As she approached the house, she couldn't shake the feeling that something was off. Was it the eerie silence that hung in the air, or the slight tremor in her gut warning her of impending danger?

"Focus," she repeated, pushing aside her doubts. "You're here for Roger, not some phantom threat."

She reached the front door and knocked, announcing her presence with authority. "Morgan Cross, FBI! I need to speak with you, Mr. Walter!"

The seconds ticked by, each one feeling like an eternity as she stood there, waiting for a response that never came. Her instincts screamed at her, urging her to act before it was too late.

"Damn it," Morgan muttered under her breath. This was no time for hesitation. She had a job to do, and she would see it through, no matter what obstacles stood in her way.

The wind rustled the leaves of the oak tree in Roger Walter's front yard, casting eerie shadows that danced across the house's façade. Morgan could hear faint movements inside – shuffling sounds and hushed whispers. She clenched her fists, fighting to keep her emotions in check. This was no time for fear or doubt; she had a mission to complete.

She raised her hand and knocked firmly on the door. "Morgan Cross, FBI!" she announced, her voice steady and commanding. "I need to speak with you, Mr. Walter!"

"J-just a minute!" came a panicked voice from behind the door. It was unmistakably Roger's, and he sounded as if he'd been caught off guard. Good. Maybe that would make him more likely to slip up and reveal something incriminating.

She knew that every second counted, but she also needed to give him the opportunity to open the door willingly. If he didn't, she'd find another way in – she always did.

As the seconds ticked by, Morgan's mind raced with possibilities. What if Roger had an accomplice? What if he'd already fled out the back door? What if he had a weapon? She shook her head, driving away the doubts.

"Mr. Walter?" she called again, her patience wearing thin. "If you don't open this door right now, I'm going to have to break it down!"

Morgan braced herself, steeling her nerves for whatever might come next. This was the moment of truth – the moment when she would finally confront the man who had been evading her. And she wouldn't let him slip through her fingers again. She couldn't.

The familiar wail of sirens approaching pierced Morgan's focus. She glanced over her shoulder and saw a fleet of police cars swarming the area, their lights flashing urgently. Among them was Derik's car, unmistakable with its black tinted windows and sleek design. A knot tightened in her stomach at the sight of him, but she knew now wasn't the time for personal grievances.

She clenched her fists, feeling the sweat slicking her palms as she prepared for whatever might be waiting on the other side.

"Roger! This is your last chance!" she shouted, pounding on the door again. "Open up or we're coming in!"

Silence answered her this time, not even a muffled shuffle from within. Morgan's heart raced as she considered the implications. Was he planning an ambush? Had he already escaped through another exit?

"Damn it," she muttered under her breath, eyes sweeping the area for any sign of movement. She could hear the officers behind her, murmuring amongst themselves as they secured the perimeter. They were good, but she'd seen firsthand how slippery her quarry was. She needed to stay one step ahead.

"Derik, get some men around back," she barked, forcing herself to push past the tension between them. "I want every inch of this property searched."

"Got it," he replied curtly, his face tight with determination as he relayed the orders to his team.

The sudden creak of a fence hinge snapped Morgan from her thoughts, and she whipped around just in time to see Roger vaulting over the wooden barrier at the back of his property. Adrenaline flooded her veins as she immediately took off after him, shouting for backup.

"Derik! He's running!" she barked into her radio, sprinting across the lawn with her gun still drawn. "Head east through the neighborhood!"

Roger was fast, but Morgan could feel her own muscles responding to the challenge, propelling her forward with every stride. The houses blurred together as she raced down narrow walkways and leaped over hedges, closing the gap between them. Her breaths came in short, ragged gasps, but she couldn't afford to slow down – not when so much was at stake.

"Stop, Roger! You can't outrun me!" she called out, her voice strained but determined. She could see him glancing back, fear etched on his face, but he didn't let up.

"Leave me alone!" he shouted back, desperation ringing clear in his tone. "I didn't do anything!"

"Then why are you running?" she shot back, her mind racing with questions. What was he hiding? Why had he lied about seeing Amy?

As they rounded a corner, Roger slipped on some wet leaves, giving Morgan the opportunity she needed to close the distance. With one final burst of speed, she lunged forward, wrapping her arms around Roger's waist and bringing him crashing to the ground. A jolt of pain surged through her body as they tumbled onto the damp grass, but she fought through it, pinning him beneath her weight.

"Enough, Roger!" she panted, her chest heaving as she tried to catch her breath. "You're under arrest!"

"Please," he begged, tears streaming down his face. "I didn't kill Amy. You have to believe me!"

Morgan's grip tightened on his wrists as she fought to suppress the flicker of doubt that threatened to creep in. She couldn't afford to waver now – not when they were so close to cracking this case.

"Tell it to the judge," she said coldly. As sirens wailed in the distance, signaling the arrival of backup, Morgan took a moment to collect herself before hoisting Roger to his feet. The chase was over, but the real battle had only just begun.

Roger's face contorted as he sobbed, his cheeks flushed and mottled with his frantic exertion. Morgan barely registered the cold sweat on her own brow as she held him firmly in place. The sound of their breaths mingling with the distant hum of traffic was almost drowned out by the pounding of her heart.

"Please, Agent Cross," Roger implored through choked sobs, "I didn't have anything to do with Amy's death. I swear!"

Morgan studied his desperate eyes, searching for any trace of deceit. Her own hardened gaze bore into him, unwavering, a testament to years of interrogating criminals. She thought of Lizzie Meadows and the poison that had taken her life, then of Amy Sanderson back at the concert hall. One false move now could cost another innocent person their life. No room for error.

"Save it, Roger," she snarled, yanking his arms behind his back and snapping the cold metal cuffs around his wrists. The sharp click echoed in the quiet suburban street, announcing the end of his freedom - if only temporarily. "You'll have plenty of time to tell your story later."

As she hauled him to his feet, Morgan caught a glimpse of concerned neighbors peering from behind curtains and screen doors. She ignored their whispers and stares, focused solely on the man whose lies had led them on this grim dance through the neighborhood.

"Let's go," she instructed tersely. With one hand gripping Roger's arm, she led him away from the scene, her thoughts racing ahead to the next steps in their investigation.

CHAPTER TEN

The fluorescent light flickered above the cold interrogation room, casting harsh shadows on the cracked linoleum floor. Morgan leaned back in her chair, one leg crossed over the other, eyes fixed on Roger Walter, who sat across from her. Derik stood beside her, arms folded, his steady gaze never leaving Roger.

"Alright, Roger," Morgan began, her voice a low growl. "You say you didn't kill Amy Sanderson. So why don't you start by telling us what really happened between the two of you?"

Roger's tear-streaked face trembled as he looked up at Morgan. He swallowed hard, his Adam's apple bobbing nervously. "It's true, I...I had an argument with Amy that night. But I swear, I didn't kill her."

"Then why lie about it?" Derik interjected, his tone sharp and accusing.

"Because..." Roger hesitated, wiping his nose with the back of his sleeve. "I was trying to get her to quit drinking. She had a...a real problem with alcohol. It was affecting her work, her relationships...everything. I just wanted to help her."

Morgan studied Roger's face, searching for any sign of deception. A part of her wanted to believe him, but she'd been burned too many times before by trusting someone. The deaths of Lizzie Meadows and the new victim weighed heavily on her conscience. If Roger wasn't their killer, then who was?

"Help her?" she mused aloud, playing with the edge of a file folder on the table. "Or control her? You lied about when you last saw her, Roger. That doesn't exactly scream 'innocent.'"

"I-I panicked!" Roger stammered, tears welling in his eyes again. "I thought if people knew we'd argued, they would blame me for her death. But I didn't kill her, Agent Cross. I swear!"

Morgan's gaze narrowed as she scrutinized Roger, her mind racing with possibilities. She'd been around liars long enough to know when someone was hiding something, and every fiber of her being told her that Roger wasn't telling the whole truth.

"Roger," Morgan began, her voice ice-cold, "You need to understand the gravity of this situation. If you don't come clean now, you could be facing some serious hard time." She leaned in closer, her eyes locked on his. "But if you confess and cooperate with us fully, I might just be able to help you."

Roger's eyes darted between Morgan and Derik, clearly feeling the pressure of their combined stares. He swallowed hard, but maintained his innocence. "I swear, Agent Cross, I didn't kill Amy. I was just trying to help her get over her alcohol problem. It was affecting her performance, and I thought if she could quit drinking, it would save her career."

Morgan's jaw clenched as she contemplated his words. The sincerity in Roger's voice was almost convincing, but she'd been fooled before. Her instincts screamed at her not to trust him, while her heart ached for the victim and her family. Inside, she waged a war between her head and her heart.

"Sometimes, people have a way of hiding things," she said evenly, her mind drifting back to her own past. "Even from themselves. Are you sure there isn't anything else you're not telling us, Roger?"

"Agent Cross, I swear on my life, I didn't kill her," he insisted, his voice cracking under the strain. "I just wanted to help her. That's all."

Morgan studied Roger's face, searching for any hint of deception in his tear-streaked features. Sweat beaded on his forehead, and he seemed to shrink under her intense gaze. Derik stepped forward, his jaw clenched as if trying to hold back a torrent of anger.

"Tell us about the security footage at the concert hall," Derik demanded. "If you're innocent, there should be something to back up your story."

Roger shook his head, his voice barely audible. "There isn't any security footage. We... we never got around to installing cameras."

"Convenient," Morgan muttered under her breath. She could feel her patience wearing thin, the frustration gnawing at her from within. Her time in prison and with the FBI had taught her that people would say anything to save themselves, and she wasn't about to let herself be fooled again.

"Is there anyone who can corroborate your alibi?" Derik asked, his eyes narrowing. "Anyone who can vouch for your whereabouts the night Amy was killed?"

"I was home alone," Roger whimpered, his voice trembling. "No one else was there."

Morgan's mind raced with thoughts and suspicions, doubts clouding her every judgment. She couldn't shake the feeling that Roger was hiding something, yet there was no concrete evidence to prove it. In the silence that followed, she could hear the echo of her own heart pounding in her chest, a relentless reminder of the stakes at hand.

Just as Morgan was about to voice her suspicions to Derik, a knock at the door interrupted her train of thought. An officer poked his head in, urgency etched on his face. "Agents Cross and Greene, I need to speak with you two."

"Make it quick," Morgan replied, her eyes never leaving Roger's defeated figure.

"Outside, please," the officer insisted, his voice strained.

Morgan exchanged a glance with Derik before they both stepped out into the hallway, leaving Roger alone in the interrogation room. As soon as the door closed behind them, the officer began to speak rapidly.

"Another body has been found," he informed them, his voice hushed but tense. "Same MO--a woman with her hands glued together, just like the other victims. It looks like our killer is still out there."

Morgan's heart skipped a beat, her stomach twisting into a tight knot. A sickening realization dawned on her: they had been wasting precious time interrogating an innocent man while the real killer remained at large.

"Where?" Morgan asked, her voice barely above a whisper.

"Suburban residence. The address is being sent to your phone right now," the officer said, handing her a slip of paper.

"Thank you," she replied tersely, forcing herself to maintain composure despite the sudden tremor in her hands. They had to act fast, retrace their steps and find the true culprit before more lives were lost.

As they hurried down the hallway, Morgan couldn't help but replay the interrogation in her mind. How could she have been so blinded by her own assumptions? The killer was still out there, and it was up to them to put an end to this twisted string of murders once and for all.

The first stop had to be the crime scene.

CHAPTER ELEVEN

Morgan stood in the doorway of the quaint suburban home, the stench of death hanging heavy in the air. She stared at the lifeless body of a woman in her forties, sprawled on the hardwood floor, her hands grotesquely glued inside oven mittens. Though there was no visible struggle, the victim's eyes were wide with terror, forever frozen in her final moments.

Derik was at the scene, along with Thomas, the cyber security expert Morgan had met earlier. Apparently, he was sticking around and working with them on this case. Several police officers were combing the scene, taking evidence photos and setting up crime scene tape.

"What the hell happened here?" Morgan asked.

"Alexa Fisher, forty-one," Thomas said, his face grim. "A neighbor came by to see her, saw her through the window and called the police... no one home but her."

Morgan's stomach bottomed out. The scene was so similar to the others, and yet different too. Why did the killer take her in her home? Was it because he knew she'd be alone at this time? The other women were killed at places they performed.

"Derik, Thomas, start searching for any evidence," Morgan instructed as they stepped into the room, their footsteps echoing through the eerily quiet house. The trio moved cautiously, their eyes scanning every inch of their surroundings.

"Looks like we've got another one," Derik muttered, his voice somber. He knelt down beside the victim's body, his gloved fingers gently probing for any possible clues.

"Same MO as the others," Thomas chimed in, studying the oven mittens that encased the woman's hands.

"Any traces of the glue used to bind the victim's hands?" Morgan asked, her voice barely masking the anger simmering within her at the thought of the killer still at large.

"Nothing yet," Derik replied, straightening up and looking around the room. "But this might be our chance to finally find a lead."

"Let's hope so," Morgan agreed, her mind racing with thoughts of how much time they had wasted on Roger. She was determined not to let her past mistakes hinder her from solving this case. If anything, it only fueled her resolve to bring the murderer to justice. The killer had eluded them for far too long, and every moment they spent searching for clues brought them closer to another potential victim. They needed to end this nightmare once and for all.

"Find anything?" she asked Derik, who was now examining the living room.

"Nothing yet," he replied, frustration evident in his voice. "But there has to be something here we can use."

"Keep looking," Morgan urged, her own determination mirrored in Derik's eyes. "We'll find something. We have to."

The front door creaked open, the sound echoing throughout the suburban home. Morgan glanced over her shoulder as a man stumbled into the foyer, his face pale and eyes wide with shock. He looked like he'd been running, sweat beading at his temples and staining his disheveled clothing.

"Who—what's going on here?" he stammered, his gaze darting between Morgan, Derik, and Thomas.

"Sir," Morgan began, stepping forward to block his view of the body in the living room. "I need you to step outside."

"Is that—No! That's my wife!" The man tried to push past her, but Morgan held him back firmly. "Please, let me see her!"

"Sir, I know this is difficult, but we need you to calm down," Morgan said softly, her voice laced with empathy. "My name is Special Agent Cross, and I'm here to help catch whoever did this. But I need your cooperation."

The man choked back a sob, tears streaming down his face. He took a deep, shuddering breath and nodded, his eyes never leaving Morgan's. "My name is Matt."

"Matt, I need you to help us. Can you tell us where you were today?" Morgan asked, her tone gentle but firm.

"I was out," Matt confessed, his voice cracking. "I haven't been a great father or husband. My kids are at daycare right now. I came as soon as I got the call that something had happened."

"Are you usually not home, Matt?" Morgan asked.

"Actually," Matt hesitated, rubbing his forehead as if trying to summon a memory. "I travel a lot for work. Sometimes I'm gone for weeks at a time, and... I've always been afraid something might happen to my family while I was away." He glanced around the room, fidgeting with his fingers. "That's why I had a secret security camera installed a while back. But honestly, I don't even know if it works anymore."

Morgan's eyes sharpened at this new piece of information. A security camera could provide them with valuable evidence — if the footage was still intact. She looked over at Thomas, who had been examining the crime scene alongside her and Derik.

"Thomas," she said, her voice all business. "Find that camera and get us whatever footage you can."

"Understood, Special Agent Cross," Thomas replied, immediately getting to work. His eyes scanned the room as he began his search for the hidden camera.

As Thomas busied himself, Morgan couldn't help but think about the implications of having a security camera in the house. If it was functional, it would be an invaluable asset to their investigation. Yet, she couldn't help but feel a tinge of unease as well. Despite her own troubled past, she understood the need for privacy and the importance of trust within a family.

"Matt," Morgan addressed him gently. "Do your wife or kids know about this camera?"

"No," Matt admitted, his gaze lowered. "I didn't want them to worry or feel like they were being watched constantly. But now..." He swallowed hard, his voice barely a whisper. "Now I wish I'd told them."

Morgan nodded solemnly, understanding the weight of regret Matt must have been feeling. As she watched Thomas move through the room, searching for the camera, she couldn't help but wonder what kind of person would target innocent people in such a cruel and calculated way. The thought sent a shiver down her spine, but she quickly pushed it away.

She looked up just in time to see Thomas examining a small, inconspicuous device mounted near the ceiling. "I found it," he called out to Morgan, his voice steady and determined.

"Good work," she praised him. "Now get us that footage."

CHAPTER TWELVE

The dimly lit room was a stark contrast to the chaos of the crime scene outside, casting eerie shadows on the walls. Morgan stood by the window, peering through the blinds at the flurry of activity beyond them. She clenched her fists tightly, trying to keep her emotions in check as she waited for Thomas to inspect the camera.

"Water damage," Thomas muttered, running his fingers over the small device in his hands. "This thing's been through the wringer."

"Can you still get the footage?" asked Morgan, her voice tight with impatience.

Thomas glanced up at her, a mischievous grin spreading across his face. "I might be able to do something..." He glanced up, eyes flashing. "if you agree to go out on a date with me."

Morgan narrowed her eyes at him, a storm of emotions swirling inside her. Part of her wanted to lash out, to demand that he take the situation seriously. But another part of her recognized the need for levity in even the darkest moments.

And besides, Thomas wasn't a bad-looking guy. Not at all.

"Really, Thomas? Now?" she snapped, her tone laced with frustration. But beneath it all, there was an undercurrent of reluctant amusement.

"Hey, can't blame a guy for trying," he replied, his grin never faltering. "But in all seriousness, I'll do my best. There has to be something we can do.""

Morgan sighed, rubbing her temples as she struggled to maintain her focus. This case was quickly spiraling out of control, and the stakes were higher than ever. She needed answers, and she needed them now.

"Look, Thomas," she said, her voice softening. "I know you're just trying to lighten the mood, but we're running out of time. If there's even a chance that this camera can give us something, anything, to work with, we have to try. People are dying."

Thomas's expression sobered, and he nodded solemnly. "I understand. I'll give it everything I've got. But I hope you'll think about my offer."

"Fix the camera," she said finally, her voice steady despite the rapid pounding of her heart. "And I'll do you one better — I won't write you up for insubordination."

"Deal," Thomas replied with a smirk, clearly unfazed by Morgan's attempt to regain control of the situation. He turned his attention back to the damaged camera, carefully prying open the casing with a set of delicate tools.

Morgan watched him work, her thoughts a whirlwind of conflicting emotions. She had spent years building up walls around herself, both in prison and after her release. Admittedly, it felt nice to be noticed, to be seen as something other than a hardened FBI agent. But she couldn't afford distractions, not now when lives were on the line and time was running out.

Morgan left the room, feeling both relieved and slightly unsettled by the brief exchange with Thomas. She needed everyone to be at their absolute best if they were going to catch the person responsible for these murders, and distractions like that could be costly.

Back in the living room, the grim sight of the victim's body greeted her once more. The woman's hands were still tightly encased in the oven mitts, glued together by some unknown substance. As she examined the gloves again, searching for any clue that might lead them closer to the killer, Derik approached her.

"Hey, Morgan," he said softly, his eyes filled with determination. "I think I might have an idea about these gloves. Follow me."

Morgan hesitated for a moment, her trust in Derik still shaken after everything they'd been through. She eyed Derik warily, the lines around her eyes deepening as she tried to gauge his sincerity. She could see a flicker of hurt flash across his face before he masked it with determination. It pained her not to trust him fully, but what other choice did she have?

"Alright," she finally said, trying to keep her voice steady. "Show me what you've got."

Derik led her through the house, his steps measured and focused. Morgan followed closely behind, her mind racing with possibilities. What had he discovered about the gloves? Could it be the breakthrough they desperately needed?

As they navigated the narrow hallway, framed family photos seemed to watch them pass — happier times now marred by tragedy. Morgan couldn't help but feel a pang of sympathy for the victim's husband and children; their lives forever changed by the actions of a heartless killer.

"Here," Derik said, turning into a small, cluttered office, where he had his laptop open. "I found an online forum for glove enthusiasts. Some of them are experts in identifying specific materials and techniques used in making gloves."

Morgan raised an eyebrow, surprised but intrigued. "And you think they could tell us something about our killer?"

"Maybe," Derik replied, a determined glint in his eye. "It's worth a shot, right?"

She nodded, unable to deny the possibility. If there was even a slim chance that this lead could bring them closer to catching the murderer, they had to explore it. "Alright, let's do it."

"Great," Derik said, opening up the forum on the laptop. "I already signed up for an account. We can post pictures of the gloves and see if anyone recognizes the material or has any other insights."

Morgan watched as Derik uploaded the images, his fingers typing with practiced ease. She couldn't help but admire his resourcefulness and determination to solve the case, even if their working relationship had been strained lately.

"Okay, it's up," Derik announced, hitting the 'post' button. "Now we wait for responses."

Morgan glanced at the screen, her heart pounding in anticipation. Would this be the breakthrough they needed? As the minutes ticked by, she found herself silently praying that one of these glove enthusiasts would recognize something important.

And maybe, just maybe, once this case was behind her, she could find a way to rebuild the trust between her and Derik – one small step at a time.

Suddenly, the sound of a notification beeped from Derik's laptop. Morgan leaned closer, her eyes scanning the reply. It was from a user named GloveExpert69, and her heart raced as Derik read the message aloud.

"This reminds me of a Steinberg piece," he said. "Steinberg?" Derik said, confused.

Morgan took out her phone and looked up 'Steinberg' online, relating it to Dallas. Her screen flooded with results, none of them concrete.

Then she typed 'Steinberg' and 'gloves.'

That brought up a more clear picture.

Photos of sculptures flooded her screen.

Sculptures of peoples' hands, pressed together--sometimes wearing gloves.

CHAPTER THIRTEEN

Morgan gripped the sides of her seat, knuckles turning white as Derik swerved through the congested city streets. Her heart pounded in her chest, adrenaline coursing through her veins.

The man they were after was Alan Steinberg, a local sculptor. And if what Morgan had seen suggested anything, then he might have something to do with the murders.

The killer's timeline was accelerating fast, and they couldn't waste any time.

"Almost there," Derik muttered, eyes darting between the road ahead and the GPS on his dashboard. "This guy's supposed to be some sort of hand sculptor or something?"

"That's what my intel suggests," Morgan replied, her voice tight with anticipation. As Derik navigated the traffic, she couldn't help but think about the victims they'd found so far: all left posed with gloves covering their hands, like some twisted signature. If this sculptor was responsible, she meant to put an end to the nightmare.

"Let's hope he's the one," Derik said, tension lacing his words. "We need a break in this case."

Morgan nodded, finding herself unable to look away from the screen of her phone as she delved deeper into the life of Alan Steinberg. His website showcased numerous images of hands in various poses, some eerily lifelike, others more abstract. But it was the sculptures adorned with gloves that sent chills down her spine. Could this really be their guy?

"Check this out," Morgan said, unable to mask the horror in her voice as she showed Derik a particularly disturbing sculpture when he stopped at a red light. It depicted two gloved hands intertwined, fingers locked together in a macabre embrace.

"Jesus," Derik murmured, eyes widening at the sight. "That's... unsettling."

"Unsettling is putting it mildly," Morgan agreed, swallowing hard before continuing her research. According to his online profile, Alan had graduated from a prestigious art school and now ran his own studio out of his home. She couldn't shake the feeling that they were on the right track, even as unease gnawed at her gut.

Morgan's thumb hovered over her phone screen, the image of gloved hands pressed together in a chillingly familiar pose making her heart race. The uncanny resemblance to the crime scenes they'd investigated gnawed at her insides like a persistent itch she couldn't reach. The artist's fixation on hands was disconcerting enough, but this particular sculpture made it difficult for Morgan to take a deep breath.

"Derik," she said, breaking the silence in the car as he stopped at another red light. "Take a look at this."

She angled the phone so that he could see the image without taking his eyes off the road for too long. Derik's brow furrowed, and he let out a low whistle. "That's... disturbing."

"Right?" Morgan tapped her phone screen, zooming in on the details. "The gloves, the way the hands are positioned... It's too damn close to what we've been finding at the scenes."

Morgan's mind raced with the possibilities - if Alan Steinberg was indeed their killer, what would that mean for the case? How many more victims might there be? And how would they bring him to justice when so much about him remained shrouded in mystery?

Morgan's fingers danced across her phone screen as she delved deeper into Alan Steinberg's background. She discovered that he had graduated from a prestigious art school and opened an independent studio where he managed to support himself entirely from the sale of his macabre sculptures. Impressive, but unsettling, given the circumstances.

"Looks like our guy has some talent," Morgan commented while scrolling through images of Steinberg's work. Derik glanced over, nodding in agreement.

"Remind me not to buy one for my living room," he quipped, earning a half-hearted chuckle from Morgan. For a moment, things between them almost felt normal--but Morgan quickly reminded herself that things between her and Derik would never be normal again.

As they approached the house, Morgan couldn't help but notice the eerie atmosphere surrounding the property. The exterior was adorned with bizarre hand sculptures, their twisted forms reaching out towards the visitors like desperate souls trapped within the confines of their metal frames. Her heartbeat quickened, sensing the weight of what they were about to uncover.

"Creepy," Derik muttered, parking the car just outside the gate.

"Understatement of the year," Morgan replied, her voice barely above a whisper. Her mind raced with thoughts of how the victims must have felt when they first encountered this place, unaware of the horror that awaited them. The anticipation was almost unbearable.

Morgan stared at the bizarre hands reaching out from the garden, grasping at the air as if trying to snatch something from it. A chill ran down her spine, but she couldn't avert her eyes.

"Keep in mind," Derik said, breaking the silence, "this guy could be eccentric. We need to be careful."

"Of course," Morgan replied, her voice steady despite the unease building inside her. "Someone with this kind of obsession... I'd expect him to be odd."

With that, they stepped out of the car, the door slamming shut behind them. The sound echoed through the quiet street. As they approached the house, the sculptures seemed to close in on them, reaching out with their cold, lifeless fingers.

"Jesus," Morgan muttered under her breath, trying to ignore the unnerving sensation of being surrounded by those hands. She focused on the front door, forcing herself to think about the task at hand.

They reached the door, and Derik raised his fist to knock. His knuckles struck the wooden surface three times, each rap resonating through the still air. They both held their breath, waiting for a response.

But there was no answer.

"Maybe he's not home?" Morgan suggested, though she doubted it. In her gut, she had a feeling that Alan Steinberg was nearby, watching them. There was a car in the driveway, after all.

"Or maybe he's just not answering," Derik countered, his eyes narrowing as he surveyed the area. "We should check around back."

"Agreed," Morgan said, her heart pounding in her chest. "Stay sharp, Derik."

"Always," he replied, offering her a tight smile before they split up, each taking a different path around the side of the house.

As she rounded the corner, Morgan couldn't shake the feeling that something was off. It wasn't just the eerie sculptures or the silence that enveloped the house - it was something deeper, more primal. Something she couldn't quite put her finger on.

Morgan's boots crunched on the gravel as she made her way to the back of the house, her eyes scanning the area for any signs of movement. The shadows cast by the twisted sculptures seemed to dance and writhe with every step she took, sending shivers down her spine.

She shook off the unease, reminding herself that eccentricities didn't automatically make someone a killer.

Reaching the back of the house, Morgan spotted a window partially obscured by overgrown ivy. Cautiously, she approached it, brushing aside the vines to get a better view of the interior.

Her heart skipped a beat as she peered through the glass - and what she saw made her blood freeze.

In the middle of the living room, a woman sat half-naked, mouth taped and tied to a chair. Long white gloves ran up her arms, eerily reminiscent of the crime scenes they had been investigating. Morgan's mind raced, a thousand thoughts colliding as she tried to process the scene before her.

"Derik, get over here!" Morgan shouted.

"Talk to me, Morgan," Derik called out as he rounded the corner, his gun drawn and at the ready.

"Look," she said, stepping aside to give him a clear view through the window. "We need to get in there right away."

"Jesus Christ," Derik breathed, his face pale with shock.

"Window," Morgan decided, her voice steady despite the turmoil churning within her. "It'll be faster, and we can't afford to waste any time."

"Got it." Derik nodded, his jaw set with determination. Together, they prepared themselves for what lay ahead, their hearts pounding in unison as they faced the unknown.

Without a second thought, Morgan swung her elbow into the window, shattering the glass with a loud crash.

CHAPTER FOURTEEN

Ignoring the sharp pain radiating from her arm, Morgan hoisted herself up and climbed through the broken window frame. She knew all too well how precious every second could be in situations like this.

As if on cue, the woman began to scream, her muffled cries filling the room as her wide eyes locked onto Morgan. The fear etched on her face was palpable, and Morgan felt her heart constrict in response. "Hold on," she called out, trying to reassure her despite the helplessness that threatened to swallow them both.

"Hey!" a deep voice boomed through the living room as a man entered, wearing a large apron splattered with what appeared to be clay or plaster. Alan Steinberg. He looked more like a mad artist than a cold-blooded killer, but Morgan wasn't about to let her guard down.

"Alan Steinberg?" Morgan demanded, her gun raised and aimed at his chest. "Step away from her, now!"

"Wh-what's going on? Who are you?" Alan stammered, his hands shaking as he held them up defensively.

"Federal agent," she replied tersely, her eyes darting between him and the terrified woman. "Untie her, slowly."

The moment Alan's eyes met Morgan's, wide with panic and surprise, his instincts kicked in. He bolted out of the room and towards the front door, leaving his half-naked girlfriend behind. The heavy apron he wore flapped wildly as he sprinted away.

"Stop!" Morgan shouted, but the sculptor was already out the door and into the yard. She followed him in hot pursuit, her heart pounding in her chest.

"Derik!" she yelled as she ran. "He's making a break for it!"

Morgan felt the adrenaline course through her veins as she chased after Alan, who was now desperately trying to get to his car. Her legs burned from the exertion, but she pushed herself harder, determined not to let him escape.

"Alan Steinberg, stop!" she called out again, but he didn't even glance back at her. His focus was entirely on reaching his vehicle and getting away from this nightmare.

She closed the distance between them. What was he hiding? Was there more to this than just a bizarre art project? She needed to catch him, to find out the truth.

As they rounded a corner, Morgan saw Alan's car parked haphazardly in the driveway. He fumbled for his keys, hands shaking violently, while Morgan continued to close the gap. Just as he opened the door and tried to slip inside, she lunged forward, grabbing onto his arm.

"Got you!" she snarled, using all her strength to try and pull him out of the car. "You're not going anywhere, Steinberg."

"Let me go!" he cried, struggling against her grip. "You don't understand! It's not what it looks like!"

"Then tell me what it is!" Morgan demanded, her voice rough with anger and exhaustion.

Despite her vice-like grip on Alan's arm, he managed to slip into the driver's seat of his car. Morgan cursed under her breath, refusing to let him escape. She lunged forward and, with a burst of adrenaline, leaped onto the hood of the car, her hands slamming against the windshield.

"Stop!" she yelled, staring directly into Alan's wide, fearful eyes. Desperation fueled her actions as much as determination; this man might be the key to solving the case that had haunted her for weeks.

Panicked, Alan slammed on the gas pedal, causing Morgan to slide across the hood. The car swerved wildly before crashing into a nearby tree with a sickening crunch. Glass from the shattered windshield rained down around her, and pain shot through Morgan's body from the impact. But she clung to consciousness, knowing that she couldn't afford to lose control now.

Derik appeared at her side, his expression a mix of concern and determination. "Morgan, are you okay?" he asked, helping her off the hood of the car.

"Never mind me," she grunted in response, wincing as she put weight on her bruised limbs. "Help me get him out of the car."

Together, they wrestled with the crumpled door, finally managing to wrench it open. Alan was dazed, blood trickling down his face from a cut on his forehead. As they hauled him out of the wreckage, Morgan couldn't help but wonder if this man – who seemed so pathetic in this moment – could really be the killer they were hunting.

"Alan Steinberg," she said coldly, leveling her gaze at him. "You're under arrest."

"Wait, you don't understand!" Alan shouted, struggling against the handcuffs. "I haven't done anything wrong!"

"Tell it to the judge," Morgan snapped, her eyes darting around the area, searching for any sign of danger or an accomplice.

"Agent Cross, wait!" a panicked voice cried out. Morgan's head whipped around to see the half-naked woman they had found inside the house racing toward them, her gloves flapping wildly as she ran. "It's not what you think!"

Morgan tensed, her hand instinctively moving toward her gun. Derik stepped protectively in front of her, his own weapon drawn and aimed at the approaching woman.

"Stop right there!" he ordered, his voice firm but controlled.

"Please, listen to me!" the woman begged, skidding to a halt, her eyes wide with terror. "This is all just a big misunderstanding! I'm his girlfriend – we were working on a new piece together."

"Is that true?" Morgan asked Alan, her gaze never leaving the woman.

"Y-yes," he stammered, his face flushed with embarrassment. "I'm an artist – I use live models for my sculptures. She was posing for me when you barged in."

Morgan exchanged a glance with Derik, trying to gauge his thoughts on the matter. Could it really be that simple? Or was this just another twisted game being played by the killer?

"Please," the woman implored, her eyes wide with sincerity. "We're not doing anything wrong. I'm his girlfriend, and I was just modeling for him. We're working on a new piece."

Morgan's grip on her gun loosened slightly, but she remained apprehensive. She couldn't afford any mistakes, not after everything they'd been through. "Prove it," she demanded, her voice firm but cautious.

"Of course," Alan said, clearly relieved to have a chance to explain himself. He led them towards the garage, the woman close behind. Morgan took note of the way she clung to Alan's arm, as if seeking comfort in his presence. Maybe there was some truth to their story after all.

The garage door creaked open, revealing a dimly lit space filled with various sculptures and tools. A single lightbulb swung gently overhead, casting eerie shadows across the rough concrete floor. Alan gestured towards a work-in-progress sculpture situated at the center of the room. It depicted the woman's hands, bound in the same manner as they had been when Morgan first spotted her.

"See?" Alan said, his voice shaky but earnest. "It's just art. We weren't doing anything illegal or dangerous."

Morgan eyed the sculpture, her mind racing with conflicting thoughts. On one hand, the artwork seemed to corroborate their claims of innocence. But on the other hand, she couldn't shake the nagging feeling that something was still amiss.

Morgan gritted her teeth, clenching her fists tightly at her sides as she stared at the myriad of hand sculptures in Alan's studio. The wasted time gnawed at her insides, a relentless reminder that the real killer was still out there. She let out a frustrated sigh, forcing herself to release the tension in her hands.

"Dammit," she muttered under her breath. *All this time spent chasing shadows, and for what? A goddamn artist with a twisted sense of beauty.*

Derik placed a hand on her shoulder, offering a sympathetic smile. "Hey, we couldn't have known. And at least now we can rule him out and move on to the next lead."

"Right," Morgan agreed, though her voice was tinged with bitterness. "But we're running out of time. Who knows what the killer could be doing right now?"

"Alan," she began, turning back to face the sculptor who had been watching them warily. "Since you're not our guy, I wonder if you'd mind taking a look at something for me?"

"Uh, sure," he replied hesitantly. "What do you need?"

"Your opinion," Morgan said bluntly, pulling up images of the gloves from the crime scenes on her phone. "These were found at both murder sites. White gloves and mittens. They seem to be significant somehow, but we just can't figure out why."

"Interesting," Alan mused, examining the images closely. His eyes narrowed in concentration, a faint furrow creasing his brow. "I'm no expert on serial killers or anything, but from an artistic perspective, I can tell you that white often symbolizes purity or innocence. Perhaps the gloves are meant to represent the victims' souls, untainted by the violence inflicted upon them?"

"Or maybe they're meant to mock the victims," Morgan suggested, her mind racing with possibilities. "To imply that they were anything but innocent."

"Could be," Alan conceded, handing the phone back to her. "But without more information, it's impossible to say for sure. Look at this," Alan said, pointing to the photos of gloves on Morgan's phone. "All these gloves are new and never worn before. See how pristine they look? That means they didn't belong to the victims."

Morgan leaned in closer, her brow furrowing as she took in his observation. He was right; each glove appeared untouched by human hands, a stark contrast to the brutalized bodies they'd been found with.

"An empty glove usually symbolizes the void of human presence," Alan continued, his eyes clouded with a mix of fascination and unease. "I think your killer is a lonesome person, potentially depressed, seeking to make a connection with others. He's trying to fill the empty space in the gloves with what's been missing from his life: companionship, women."

Morgan considered the implications of his words, her mind racing with possibilities. It made sense, but it also complicated things. How could they possibly track down a suspect who so desperately clung to the shadows?

"Any idea how we might catch someone like that?" she asked, her voice tinged with frustration.

Alan shook his head, the faintest hint of a smile tugging at the corner of his mouth, as if he admired the killer's twisted artistry. "Probably not. He's learned to live in the shadows, blend into the background. And that's where he'll remain."

"Dammit," Morgan muttered under her breath, her fingers clenching around her phone. She knew they were running out of time, and the thought of another victim suffering at the hands of this sadistic killer made her blood boil.

"Every bit of information helps," Derik said, placing a reassuring hand on her shoulder. "We'll keep digging, and sooner or later, we'll find him."

As they left the artist's house, Morgan couldn't shake the image of those pristine gloves, the eerie emptiness they represented. She knew they were dealing with a phantom, a man who lurked in the darkest corners of society, and she couldn't help but wonder if they'd ever be able to drag him into the light.

CHAPTER FIFTEEN

Morgan's thoughts were still consumed by the chilling conversation with Alan Steinberg when she and Derik returned to the precinct. She couldn't help but feel a sense of dread creeping up her spine, knowing that they were dealing with a killer who was a master at hiding in plain sight. As they walked through the bustling office, she noticed Thomas leaning against a desk, a triumphant glint in his eyes.

"Hey, you two," he called out, motioning for them to come over. "Got some good news for a change. Managed to salvage some footage from that ruined drive we found."

"Really?" Morgan said, her interest piqued. "What does it show?"

"Let's head to the tech room and find out," Thomas replied, leading the way.

The dimly lit tech room smelled faintly of coffee and stale air, a familiar scent that never failed to make Morgan feel like she was at home. They gathered around a large monitor, anticipation building as Thomas prepared to play the footage.

"Alright, this is from the last time the camera was functional at Alexa Fischer's house," he explained. "It's from about three months ago."

As the grainy video started playing, Morgan felt her heart pounding in her chest. Could this be the breakthrough they needed? The image on the screen showed a seemingly ordinary day at the victim's house: people coming and going, birds chirping in the trees. But then, something caught her eye.

"Wait," she said, her voice barely more than a whisper. "Pause it there."

Thomas obliged, freezing the frame as Morgan leaned in closer, her pulse racing. She could feel the weight of Derik's gaze on her, his curiosity palpable.

"See that?" she asked, pointing at a figure in the background, partially obscured by the shadows. "That's our guy. He's been watching her for months."

"Damn," Derik muttered, his eyes widening with surprise. "Nice catch, Morgan."

"Thanks," she replied, her mind already racing ahead, trying to piece together the puzzle. How had he managed to stay hidden for so long? Was he watching their every move, waiting for the perfect moment to strike?

"Let's keep digging," Thomas said, sensing her determination. "There has to be more we can find."

The footage continued to play, revealing a man entering Alexa's home, his face hidden by the brim of his hat. Their body language spoke volumes, and Morgan felt a sinking feeling in her gut as she realized what she was witnessing.

Alexa Fischer had been having an affair.

Another victim with a secret life, just like Amy Sanderson. And Lizzie Meadows's secret past, how her bullying had led to another person's suicide--it seemed all of these women had something to hide, even if there were stark differences between them.

"Thomas," Morgan said, rubbing her temples, "can you send me all the relevant footage? I need to have a talk with Matt Fischer."

"Of course," Thomas replied, already working on transferring the files.

***

As Morgan pulled up to the Fischer residence, she noticed yellow police tape crisscrossing the front door, a grim reminder of the tragedy that had unfolded within. Officers walked in and out of the house, still collecting evidence while others guarded the perimeter. Morgan spotted Matt sitting on the front porch, his hands clasped together as he stared at the ground.

"Matt," Morgan called out, approaching him cautiously. "I need to speak with you."

He looked up, his eyes red-rimmed and tired. "What is it now, Agent Cross?"

"Can we talk somewhere private?" she asked softly, not wanting to draw attention from the other officers nearby.

"Sure," he said, standing up and leading her around the side of the house, away from prying eyes.

"Matt, I'm afraid I've found something in the security footage that you should be aware of," Morgan began, hesitating for a moment before continuing. "It appears that Alexa had been seeing someone else."

Matt's eyes widened, and he looked away, struggling to process the information. "You're saying... my wife was having an affair?"

Morgan nodded solemnly. "I'm sorry, Matt. But it's important that we investigate every aspect of Alexa's life to find her killer."

"Who was it?" Matt asked, his voice barely audible, the pain evident in his eyes.

"We don't know yet," Morgan admitted. "The man's face was obscured in the footage, but we're working on identifying him."

"Another secret," Matt muttered, shaking his head. "How could I have missed it?"

"Matt, don't blame yourself for Alexa's choices," Morgan advised gently. "Our focus right now is to catch her killer."

"No," Matt said, shaking his head in disbelief. "This can't be true. We were happy. I would have known if she was seeing someone else. I know I was gone for work a lot, but... but I did it for us!"

"Sometimes people hide things, even from those closest to them," Morgan replied gently. Her thoughts drifted back to her own past – the false accusations, the time spent in prison – and she knew all too well how secrets could destroy lives.

Matt shook his head in disbelief, trying to come to terms with the news. "I just... I can't believe it. How could she do this to me?"

Matt looked up at her, his eyes red and pleading. "Please, Agent Cross. Find out who did this. I need to know the truth."

"We will," Morgan promised, her resolve strengthening. "I won't stop until we have answers."

As she rose from the steps, Morgan couldn't help but feel a pang of sympathy for the broken man beside her. Yet, in the back of her mind, she knew that she had to keep an eye on him as well. Grief and shock could make people unpredictable, and she couldn't afford any surprises in her pursuit of justice.

Morgan stepped away from Matt's home, the weight of the conversation still pressing heavily on her. The wind picked up as she walked down the driveway, rustling the leaves and tossing her dark hair across her face. She scanned the area for the officer she'd requested earlier.

"Officer Jenkins," she called out, spotting the young man in uniform standing by a patrol car. He looked up, his eyes filled with determination.

"Special Agent Cross," he acknowledged with a nod, stepping forward to meet her halfway.

"Listen, I need you to watch Matt Fischer closely," Morgan instructed, her voice firm but laced with concern. "Make sure he doesn't leave town or do anything suspicious. We can't afford any missteps right now."

"Understood, ma'am," Officer Jenkins replied, accepting the responsibility without hesitation.

"Good," Morgan replied with a curt nod, the professional mask she'd perfected over the years slipping back into place. "Keep me informed of any developments."

"Will do, Agent Cross," Jenkins assured her, before turning back towards the house to assume his post.

Morgan sighed, feeling a sudden weariness settle into her bones. Exhaustion was creeping its way through her body, an inevitable side effect of the endless hours spent chasing shadows and digging through secrets. She rubbed her temples, trying to stave off the headache that threatened to bloom behind her eyes.

As she made her way back to her car, Morgan couldn't shake the feeling that something was amiss. Out of the corner of her eye, she caught a glimpse of movement amongst the trees across the street. Squinting, she tried to discern if someone was hiding there, watching her.

"Get it together, Cross," she muttered under her breath, chiding herself for letting paranoia get the best of her. She was just exhausted, that was all.

Shaking her head, Morgan climbed into her car and started the engine. As she pulled away from the curb, she cast one last glance at the trees, but saw nothing out of the ordinary. With a sigh, she refocused her attention on the road ahead, determined to catch the monster responsible for these heinous crimes. For now, she needed to get back to the precinct and figure out their next move.

CHAPTER SIXTEEN

Morgan's fingers drummed impatiently on the edge of the table in the briefing room, the staccato rhythm echoing through the nearly empty precinct. It was getting later in the day, but the fluorescent lights overhead cast a harsh glare on the stacks of case files scattered in front of her. She fixated on the photos of the victims, all young women with dark secrets they thought they had successfully buried. Morgan narrowed her eyes and muttered to herself, "He always picks them for their secrets, doesn't he?"

"Seems that way," Derik replied, slipping into the chair across from her. He looked tired, his normally sharp green eyes dulled by exhaustion. "It's like he wants control over them, even after they're dead."

"Control," Morgan repeated, tasting the word in her mouth as if it were a key to a hidden lock. She scrutinized the evidence, searching for any pattern that could reveal the killer's true motive. "Each victim had something to hide, something that made them vulnerable. That's what he preys on – vulnerability."

"Exactly." Derik leaned forward, resting his elbows on the table. "But how does he find out about their secrets? And why go through all this trouble to kill them?"

"Maybe it's not just about killing them," Morgan mused, her voice low. "Maybe he wants to prove that he's smarter, more powerful than everyone else. That he can uncover anyone's secrets and use them against them."

"Sounds like one hell of an ego," Derik said, his lips curling into a grim smile.

"Or one hell of a psychopath," Morgan countered. She sighed, rubbing her temples as if to chase away the throbbing ache behind her eyes. "Either way, we need to figure out how he's choosing his targets and stop him before he claims another life."

"Agreed. So, what's the plan?"

Morgan leaned back in her chair, her gaze drifting to the evidence board on the far wall. Among the many disturbing items collected from the crime scenes, one piece of evidence stood out to her – the gloves.

Each victim had been found wearing them. Different styles, but all with that poisonous glue.

"Those damn gloves," she muttered, rising from her seat. "There has to be something about them we're missing. Some clue that'll lead us straight to him."

"Could be," Derik agreed, following her lead as they made their way through the maze of desks and filing cabinets. "But what makes you think there's more to find?"

"Call it intuition," Morgan said, her voice quiet but resolute. "We've been overlooking something, I just know it. And if we can figure out what it is, maybe we can finally put an end to this nightmare."

As they walked toward the evidence room, Morgan couldn't help but let her thoughts drift. She knew that the key to solving the case lay within those gloves, but how? The victims' secrets held the power the killer sought, but the gloves... they were his signature, his twisted calling card. What other purpose could they serve?

***

The door to the evidence room creaked open, revealing rows of shelves packed with boxes and bags meticulously labeled and catalogued. The room was dimly lit, casting shadows on the walls. Morgan and Derik stepped inside, greeted by a young employee who nodded in recognition.

"Agent Cross, Agent Greene," the employee said, his voice slightly trembling. "What can I help you find?"

"We need to see the gloves from the recent homicide cases," Morgan replied, her voice steady but firm.

"Of course," the man responded, leading them deeper into the room. He stopped before a large metal cabinet and fumbled with the key for a moment before swinging the doors open. "Here they are," he said, gesturing toward a row of sealed plastic bags, each containing a single glove.

"Thanks," Morgan said, dismissing him with a curt nod. The employee left, and Morgan and Derik were alone with the chilling evidence.

"Hand me the tongs, will you?" she asked, slipping on a pair of latex gloves. Derik handed her the requested tool, and she carefully picked up the first bag, studying its contents.

"White glove from Lizzie Meadows, the pageant queen," Morgan read aloud, her brow furrowing as she examined the delicate lace fabric. "Such a stark contrast to the brutality of her death."

"Maybe that's the point," Derik suggested, watching her closely. "These gloves don't belong in a crime scene. They're out of place, just like the secrets these women kept."

Morgan's eyes narrowed as she considered his words, turning the bag over in her hand. "You might be onto something. But we still need to find the connection between the gloves and the killer."

"Right," Derik agreed, his gaze never leaving Morgan's face. "Let's keep looking."

As Morgan continued to examine the glove, her mind raced with possibilities. The killer had chosen these gloves for a reason, but what was it? What message was he trying to send? And most importantly, how could she use this information to track him down and put an end to his reign of terror?

"Hey, Morgan," Derik said, breaking her thoughts. "I know you're onto something here, but remember, we're a team. We'll figure this out together."

"Thanks, Derik," Morgan replied softly, grateful for his support but still uneasy about the secrets that lay between them. For now, though, they had a case to solve—and a killer to catch.

Morgan carefully turned the white glove inside out, her eyes scanning every inch of the delicate fabric for any clues. The room seemed to hold its breath as she worked, the hum of the overhead fluorescent lights the only sound accompanying her movements.

"Wait," she whispered, pausing as her eyes locked onto a small detail that hadn't been visible before. It was a tiny stitched monogram, almost imperceptible amid the intricate lace patterns. "Derik, look at this."

"Where?" he asked, leaning in closer to examine the glove with her.

"Here," Morgan pointed out, her gloved finger hovering just above the minuscule letters. "See those stitches? That's a monogram, or some kind of signature. It looks almost like... a series of arrows."

"Interesting," Derik mused, his brow furrowing. "Killers sometimes leave calling cards like this. But what does it stand for?"

"I don't know yet," Morgan admitted, feeling a renewed sense of determination. This clue could be the key to understanding the killer's motive and ultimately stopping him. "Let's take this to the briefing room and see if we can find any matches for this symbol."

CHAPTER SEVENTEEN

In the briefing room, Morgan sat at a computer, her fingers flying over the keyboard as she conducted a reverse image search on the mysterious monogram. Derik paced behind her, trying to keep his mind occupied while they waited for the results.

"Anything?" he asked after several minutes had passed.

"Nothing," Morgan sighed, frustration creeping into her voice. "No matches for this symbol. It's like it doesn't exist."

"Maybe it's something personal to the killer," Derik offered, attempting to help. "A family crest, or some sort of secret organization?"

"Could be," Morgan conceded, her mind racing with possibilities. She knew they were close to unraveling the truth, but this monogram remained stubbornly elusive. "We're missing something, Derik. We just need to figure out what it is."

"Let's take a step back," Derik suggested, placing a reassuring hand on her shoulder. "We'll find the answer, Morgan. We always do."

Morgan stared at the computer screen. The search bar blinked mockingly, a cruel reminder of the countless failed attempts to find any information on the monogram. Her fingers hovered over the keyboard, ready to type in yet another combination of keywords.

"Maybe we're going about this the wrong way," Derik said, leaning against the table next to her. "We could try researching different types of monograms, see if that leads us anywhere."

"Maybe." Morgan's voice was flat, her mind churning with frustration and growing desperation. Time was running out, and they still had nothing solid to go on.

Derik fell silent, watching her intently. She could feel his eyes on her, heavy with unspoken thoughts. Morgan knew what he wanted to say, but she wasn't ready to have that conversation—not now, when there was so much at stake.

"Look, Morgan—" he started, only for her to cut him off.

"Save it, Derik. We can talk later. Right now, let's focus on finding this killer."

"Fine," he muttered. "But at some point, we're going to have to address the damn elephant in the room."

Morgan turned back to the computer, her stomach twisting with both relief and bitterness. They needed to work together, at least for now. But she couldn't forget, couldn't forgive his betrayal. Not yet.

Morgan typed in another set of keywords, her pulse quickening as new images filled the screen. Maybe this time, they would find something—some clue that would lead them to the truth.

And as she continued her search, Morgan couldn't help but wonder if they would ever be able to mend the fractured bond between them. Or if it was simply too broken, destined to splinter further with every passing day.

The tension in the room was palpable as Morgan continued to sift through the seemingly endless string of search results, her fingers tapping impatiently on the desk. The silence between her and Derik was suffocating, but she refused to be the one to break it. She had every right to be mad at him, and until he made things right, she wasn't going to let that anger fade.

"Look, Morgan," Derik finally spoke up, his voice hesitant and a little shaky. "I just wanted to say... I'm sorry."

Morgan's fingers froze on the keyboard, but she didn't look away from the screen. Her jaw clenched, and she could feel the anger boiling under her skin. Still, she said nothing, waiting for him to continue.

"I thought I told you to save it for later," she said.

"Well, I don't want to," he told her. "I want things to go back to the way they were before," he admitted, his eyes searching her face for any sign of forgiveness. "I know I messed up, but we were a great team once. I miss that."

She couldn't ignore him any longer. With a sigh, she turned to face him, her gaze icy. "There's only one way to do that, Derik," she said, her voice low and steady. "Help me find the people who put me in prison. Give me all the information you've got."

His expression tightened, and she could see the reluctance in his eyes. But she wouldn't budge. This was non-negotiable.

Just then, Morgan's phone buzzed in her pocket, the sudden vibration jolting her back into reality. Derik watched as she pulled it out and glanced at the screen, her face a mask of professionalism. She swiped to answer the call, her eyes never leaving his.

"Cross," she said curtly, her voice sharp and authoritative.

"Agent Cross, it's Officer Jenkins," came the voice on the other end. "I'm watching Matt, like you asked. Nothing unusual to report so far. But there is something that caught my attention."

"Go on," she prompted, her grip on the phone tightening.

"An unfamiliar man has been spotted in the neighborhood a couple of times, wearing gloves even though it's been hot outside. I asked around, but none of the neighbors recognize him or claim he lives here."

"Did you get a photo?"

"Sending it to you now," Jenkins replied.

As Morgan waited for the image to come through, she could feel Derik's gaze on her, his curiosity piqued by the conversation. She knew he was itching to ask what was going on, but she couldn't bring herself to include him just yet. Trust had to be earned, after all.

Her phone buzzed again, signaling the arrival of the picture. She opened the message and studied the image, her brow furrowing in concentration. The man in question appeared unassuming, but there was something unsettling about the way he wore gloves in the summer heat. Morgan studied the photo intently, taking in every detail of the man's appearance. The hoodie was pulled low over his face, casting a shadow that obscured his features, but it couldn't hide the strangeness of those gloved hands hanging at his sides. Something about the image sent a shiver down her spine.

"Jenkins," she said into her phone, her voice sharp and commanding, "I want you to find this guy and bring him in for questioning."

"Understood, Agent Cross. We'll track him down."

As Morgan ended the call, she found herself staring at the photo again. Who was this man? And why was he lurking around the victim's house with gloves in the sweltering heat? Her instincts told her that there was more to his story than met the eye.

She glanced up from the photo and noticed Derik watching her, concern etched on his face. Despite everything that had happened between them, she knew he still cared. But it wasn't enough. Not yet.

"Derik," Morgan said, her voice tense and strained, "if you want to help, see if you can find out what this symbol means. I'm going to take a quick break while we wait for Jenkins."

Without waiting for his response, she turned on her heel and left the room, her steps echoing through the quiet hallway.

CHAPTER EIGHTEEN

The break room was dimly lit, casting shadows on the plain white walls that were adorned with outdated posters about workplace safety. The hum of the fluorescent lights above seemed to heighten the tension that hung in the air like a thick fog. Morgan approached the coffee machine, her hands trembling slightly as she reached for a stale Styrofoam cup.

"Come on, Morgan," she whispered to herself, willing the machine to dispense the dark liquid faster. "You've been through worse. You can handle this."

As the bitter aroma filled her nostrils, she tried to focus on the warmth of the cup between her hands, to allow it to ground her in the present moment. But her mind refused to cooperate, instead replaying fragments of memories and half-formed thoughts, each one more unsettling than the last.

Is this really what I've become? she wondered, her gaze fixed on the swirling patterns in her cup. *A woman who can't even trust her own partner? I said I wanted to work alone... I should've stuck to it.*

She shook her head, trying to dislodge the unwelcome thoughts that threatened to pull her under. This wasn't the time for introspection – not when there was a killer out there, stalking his next victim.

Taking a deep breath, Morgan raised the cup to her lips and took a tentative sip. The hot liquid scalded her tongue, but the pain was almost welcome; it served as a reminder that she was still alive, still fighting.

The sound of footsteps echoed through the break room, pulling Morgan's attention away from her coffee. She looked up to find Thomas standing in the doorway, his warm smile contrasting sharply with the cold dread that had settled in her chest.

"Hey, Morgan," he greeted her, his voice light and friendly. "Taking a break?"

"Something like that," she replied, forcing a smile onto her face. It felt strange, almost unnatural, after everything that had happened, but she couldn't deny the small measure of comfort it provided.

Thomas stepped further into the room, his movements fluid and effortless. "I've been reviewing security footage from around where the victims have been found," he said, his expression turning serious. "No luck yet, though."

Morgan's heart sank at the news. She had been clinging to the hope that they might find some clue, some connection between the victims that would lead them to their killer. But as the hours ticked by, that hope was beginning to slip through her fingers like sand.

"Thanks for trying," she told him, her words genuine despite the hollowness that accompanied them. Deep down, she knew that Thomas was doing everything he could to help her – even going above and beyond what was expected of him. And while she didn't want to admit it, she found herself grateful for his support.

"Of course," he replied, his eyes meeting hers with an intensity that took her breath away. Thomas shifted on his feet, the smile on his face never faltering. "So, listen, I know we've both been incredibly busy with this case, but I have to ask again – when are you going to let me take you out on that date?" he asked, a hint of playfulness in his voice.

Morgan hesitated for a moment, her mind racing. She knew it wasn't fair to lead him on – not when she was still so tangled up in her own emotions and unresolved issues, especially with Derik. But the offer was tempting--almost as tempting as what she could gain from Thomas's unique skill set.

He was a cyber security expert, after all. He might be able to help her find out about who framed her.

On one hand, she recognized that Thomas could potentially help her uncover the truth about her father's time at the FBI, as well as who had framed her for murder all those years ago. His hacking skills were unparalleled, and she couldn't deny that there was a part of her that wanted – needed – to know the answers to the questions that had haunted her for so long.

But on the other hand, she couldn't shake the feeling that using Thomas for his abilities would be wrong. He was clearly into her, and she didn't want to take advantage of his feelings just to satisfy her own curiosity and thirst for justice. The guilt gnawed at her insides, making her stomach churn with unease.

Morgan's gaze flicked between the coffee machine and Thomas, the steam from her cup mingling with her conflicting thoughts. Taking a deep breath, she made her decision.

"Thomas," she began, turning to face him fully. "I'll think about your offer, but right now, I need to focus on the case." She hesitated before adding, "I can't promise anything more."

A grin spread across his face, his eyes lighting up like stars in the night sky. "That's fine by me, Morgan. I can wait for the right person. Just let me know if you change your mind."

"Thank you," she replied, relieved that he didn't seem offended or hurt by her response. She took a sip of her coffee, allowing the bitter liquid to ground her thoughts and bring her back to the present moment.

The sound of the break room door creaking open caught her attention, and Morgan glanced over to see Derik entering the room, his brow furrowed as he surveyed the scene before him. His eyes locked onto Thomas, and something dark flashed in their depths.

"Excuse me," Derik said curtly, his voice barely concealing the anger simmering beneath the surface. He directed his glare at Thomas, who seemed to understand the unspoken message.

"Of course," Thomas replied, raising his hands in surrender. "I'll just… go get back to work." With one last lingering look at Morgan, he turned on his heel and left the room, leaving her alone with Derik.

Morgan frowned, watching as Derik approached her with an air of determination, his footsteps echoing on the tiled floor. She couldn't shake the feeling that whatever conversation they were about to have would only add fuel to the fire that had been burning between them since her return.

She mentally prepared herself for another confrontation, taking a slow, deliberate sip of her coffee as Derik came to a stop in front of her. She could feel his eyes boring into her, searching for answers she wasn't sure she wanted to give.

"Derik," she said quietly, steeling herself for the storm she knew was brewing. "Let's just focus on the case."

Morgan turned back to the coffee machine, her hands shaking slightly as she poured herself another cup. The hot liquid splashed against the sides of the mug, and she tried to ignore the tension radiating from Derik's rigid stance beside her.

"Really, Morgan?" he asked through gritted teeth, his voice barely more than a growl. "You're seriously thinking about going on a date with that guy?"

Morgan felt her anger rising like steam from her coffee. She didn't appreciate being spied on, especially by someone who had betrayed her trust in the past. She shot him a glare and narrowed her eyes. "First of all, I never said I was going on a date with him. I said I'd think about it."

"Whatever," he scoffed, crossing his arms over his chest. "It's not like you have great judgment when it comes to men."

"Excuse me?" Morgan set her mug down on the counter with a little more force than necessary, causing coffee droplets to splash onto the countertop. "That's rich coming from you, Derik."

"Hey, I'm just trying to look out for you," he retorted defensively, his eyes narrowing.

"Since when is eavesdropping 'looking out for me'? Last time I checked, my personal life is none of your business." She knew she should be focusing on the case, but the fury bubbling inside her wouldn't let her walk away from this fight. Not yet.

Derik's jaw tightened, and for a moment, he seemed lost for words. His gaze bore into her, a mixture of hurt and frustration flickering behind his stormy eyes. "Just because we've had our differences doesn't mean I don't still care about you, Morgan."

"Then show it by respecting my privacy and staying out of my personal life," she said through clenched teeth.

"Fine," he snapped, throwing his hands up in defeat. "You want me to stay out of it? I will."

"Good." Morgan grabbed her coffee and turned away from him, not wanting to give him the satisfaction of seeing how much this confrontation had rattled her. She could feel his eyes on her as she left the room, but she refused to look back. There was a killer to catch, and no amount of personal drama was going to stand in her way.

The coffee machine sputtered to life, filling the air with the bitter scent of freshly brewed java. Morgan's hands trembled slightly as she gripped her cup, feeling the heat seep through the thin cardboard and into her skin. She needed that warmth, that liquid courage to steady herself after the heated exchange with Derik.

"Special Agent Cross," a young officer called out, interrupting the tense silence between her and Derik. He stood in the doorway, his uniform crisp and a folder clutched in his hand. "Your suspect is in the interrogation room, waiting."

Morgan met Derik's gaze, her expression hardening. "We'll finish this later," she told him, taking a deep breath to calm her nerves. "Right now, I have a killer to catch."

She strode past the young officer, her heels clicking against the linoleum floor with purpose. The precinct was abuzz with activity, but all she could hear was the pounding of her own heart and the thoughts racing through her mind. Was this really the man responsible for the gruesome murders? Would they finally bring justice to those innocent victims?

As Morgan approached the interrogation room, she took a moment to gather her thoughts. She couldn't let her personal issues with Derik cloud her judgment. This was too important. She had to be focused, relentless, and unyielding. She glanced down at her coffee, the swirling darkness within mirroring the storm brewing inside her. With a decisive nod, she set the cup aside and marched into the interrogation room, ready to face whatever lay ahead.

CHAPTER NINETEEN

Morgan entered the interrogation room, her eyes immediately drawn to the man seated in front of her. His simple appearance belied his age – a man in his fifties with a graying beard and unkempt hair. She couldn't help but notice the gloves he wore, an odd accessory that seemed out of place in the sterile environment.

"Joe Dancer," she said under her breath, glancing down at the file in her hands. According to the information within, Joe had no criminal record and recently worked at a local bar. On paper, he didn't seem like the type to commit such heinous acts. But then again, monsters often hid behind unassuming masks.

"Agent Cross," Joe greeted her, his voice gravelly from years of hard living. "Do you mind if I keep my gloves on? Occupational habit."

"Go ahead," Morgan replied, her tone cool and detached. She needed to remain impartial, to see him as just another suspect rather than the potential key to unlocking this twisted mystery.

"Thanks," Joe replied, flexing his gloved fingers. "I appreciate it."

Morgan fixed her gaze on him, studying his every movement, searching for any sign of deception. It was time to probe deeper, to peel away the layers and find the truth that lurked beneath.

"Mr. Dancer," she began, the words tasting like ash on her tongue. "You've been brought in today because your presence has been noted near the scenes of a recent murder. We need to establish your connection, if any, to this crime."

"Murder?" Joe's eyes widened, genuine shock registering on his weathered face. "I swear, Agent Cross, I don't know anything about that. I'm just a barback, washing glasses and mopping up spillage."

Morgan leaned forward, her eyes narrowing as she scrutinized his expression. Was he telling the truth, or was he merely a skilled liar? She couldn't be sure. Not yet.

"Where were you last night?" she asked, testing his alibi.

"Working at the bar," Joe answered without hesitation. "Double shifts each night. You can check with my boss if you don't believe me."

Morgan's mind raced as she considered her next move. It would be easy to dismiss him, to chalk it up to coincidence and let him walk free.

But something in her gut told her there was more to this man than met the eye.

"Mr. Dancer," she said, her voice steady despite the turmoil within her. "If you're innocent, then you have nothing to fear. But I need your full cooperation if we're going to get to the bottom of this. Are you willing to help?"

"Of course, Agent Cross," Joe replied, his eyes meeting hers. "I want to see this killer brought to justice as much as you do."

"Good." Morgan allowed herself a small, grim smile. "Then let's get to work."

Morgan eyed the man sitting across from her. Joe Dancer, with his quiet indifference, seemed unfazed by the sterile interrogation room and the harsh fluorescent lighting that cast stark shadows on his face. His hands, clad in black gloves, were clasped together on the table in front of him, his posture rigid yet relaxed. Morgan had interrogated countless suspects over the years, but something about Joe's eerie calm unnerved her.

"Your presence in the neighborhood where the latest victim was found is... suspicious, to say the least," Morgan pressed, gauging his reaction. But Joe remained impassive, his icy blue eyes never leaving hers.

"Actually," he said, tilting his head ever so slightly, "it's quite simple. You see, my piano teacher lives in that area. I visit her twice a week for lessons."

Morgan raised an eyebrow. Piano lessons? It seemed like an odd hobby for someone who wore gloves all the time. Yet, she couldn't deny the possibility that it could be true. Nothing about Joe screamed 'killer' – at least, not yet. She knew better than to judge a book by its cover, though. After all, she'd been framed for murder ten years ago, and she'd spent the last decade working to clear her name and regain her position as an FBI agent.

"Interesting," she mused, crossing her arms. Morgan studied Joe's gloved hands, the black fabric stark against the cold metal table. A pianist who wore gloves constantly seemed like a contradiction, and she couldn't help but wonder what would drive someone to play through the pain of an apparent rash.

"Joe," she began, her voice steady, "you wear these gloves all the time because of a skin condition, yet you've chosen piano as your hobby. Most people would find that odd."

Joe's calm demeanor didn't waver, the corners of his lips curling into a small smile. "My mother loved the piano," he said, flexing his fingers beneath the fabric. "I learned to play in her honor, despite my condition. The pain... it's a reminder of her, I suppose."

There was something about the way he spoke that made Morgan feel uneasy. Was he genuinely sentimental or hiding something more sinister? She shook off the thought and focused on the task at hand.

"Who is this piano teacher of yours?" she asked, pen poised above her notepad.

"Betty Garner," Joe replied. "She's been teaching me for years now. You can call her if you need to verify my story. She'll tell you everything you want to know."

Morgan jotted down Betty's name, making a mental note to follow up on his claim. Joe's eyes never left hers, the challenge in his gaze unwavering. She knew she needed to tread carefully – one wrong move could send the killer into hiding for good.

"Alright, Joe, I'll do just that," she said, meeting his stare head-on. "And if your alibi checks out, then we can put this matter to rest. But if it doesn't... well, let's just say you'd better hope it does. I'll be right back."

As she stood up from the table, Morgan's mind raced with questions. Was Joe Dancer a misunderstood pianist, or was he the ruthless killer she'd been hunting for weeks? Only time – and Betty Garner's testimony – would tell.

***

Morgan stared at the phone in her hand, her fingers tapping a restless rhythm against its hard plastic surface. She hesitated, questioning her own instincts about Joe Dancer. But with no concrete evidence to hold him, she had little choice but to make the call.

"Alright," she murmured to herself, "let's see what you have to say, Betty Garner."

She dialed the number Joe had given her and waited, listening to the monotonous ringing on the other end. Her heart beat a little faster, anticipation and doubt warring within her.

"Hello?" The voice on the other end was soft and warm, like a grandmother's embrace.

"Betty Garner?" Morgan asked, steeling herself for the conversation.

"Yes, dear. Who might this be?"

"Special Agent Morgan Cross, FBI. I'm investigating a series of crimes, and I need to ask you some questions about one of your students, Joe Dancer."

"Joe? Oh, he's such a nice young man," Betty replied, her tone genuine and kind. "I've been teaching him piano for years now. What can I help you with, Agent Cross?"

"Ms. Garner, I need to know if Joe was with you last night during his scheduled piano lesson."

"Indeed, he was," Betty confirmed, her voice filled with certainty. "He comes twice a week, you see, and we were working on a particularly difficult piece last night. Why do you ask? Is something wrong?"

Morgan shifted her weight, digging her heel into the worn carpet beneath her feet. She needed to tread lightly here, to avoid raising any unnecessary alarm. So far, everything Joe had said to Morgan seemed to be true.

"Ms. Garner, I don't want to cause you any undue concern, but we're looking into a matter that involves Joe's whereabouts last night. It's important that we verify his alibi."

"Alibi?" Betty's voice trembled with concern. "Oh, my goodness. I assure you, Agent Cross, Joe was here with me until well into the evening. He's had such a hard life, what with his hands and all... I couldn't imagine him ever getting mixed up in anything dangerous."

Morgan closed her eyes for a moment, taking in Betty's words. She could feel a pang of sympathy tugging at her, but she knew she needed to remain objective.

"Ms. Garner, can you tell me what time Joe left your house last night?" Morgan asked, her voice steady and professional.

"Of course, dear. If I recall correctly, it was around eight in the evening," Betty replied, her voice reflecting a genuine concern for Joe's welfare.

Morgan's brow furrowed as she calculated the timeline in her head. The murders had occurred between nine and eleven p.m., which meant that Joe could have potentially been out in time to commit them. She couldn't ignore this possibility, despite the heartache she sensed in Betty's voice.

"Ms. Garner," she began, her voice steady and authoritative, "has Joe ever exhibited any violent tendencies? Anything at all that would cause you concern?"

Betty's laughter rang out through the phone, jarring in its sincerity. "Violent tendencies? Oh, no, dear, not at all. Joe is as harmless as they come. He's just a misunderstood young man with a rare condition on his hands." A hint of sadness crept into her voice as she continued, "The world can be so cruel to people like him."

Morgan felt an unexpected pang of sympathy for Joe as she listened to Betty's words. She stared at the suspect seated across from her, watching him fidget with the gloves on his rash-covered hands. His alibi was plausible; he had been attending piano lessons with Betty until eight p.m., and he hadn't been anywhere near the crime scene. There was no connection between him and the other murder victims.

Despite her hardened exterior, Morgan found herself wanting to believe in Joe's innocence. The thought of such a gentle soul becoming entangled in a brutal murder investigation was unsettling. But the truth had to be her priority, and she couldn't let her emotions sway her judgment.

"Thank you, Ms. Garner," Morgan said, trying to keep her voice neutral. "Your information has been very helpful."

"Is there anything else I can do for you, dear?" Betty asked, genuine concern evident in her tone.

"Nothing at the moment, but I might be in touch if we need further information. Thank you again for your cooperation," Morgan replied before ending the call.

With a sigh of resignation, Morgan thanked Betty and hung up the phone. She stared at it for a moment, her fingertips still resting on the cool, smooth surface, as if she could somehow bring a connection to the real killer into existence. But Joe Dancer seemed to be nothing more than another dead-end.

Which meant the real killer was still out there, and she was wasting more time.

CHAPTER TWENTY

The sun dipped lower in the sky, casting long shadows across the precinct's parking lot as Morgan leaned against her car, defeated. The chill of the metal seeped through her jacket, but she barely noticed. Her mind was consumed with frustration over the time she'd wasted with Joe Dancer.

Another dead end. She felt as if she were trying to navigate a labyrinth with no exit, each turn leading to another brick wall. It was maddening.

"Hey, Cross."

Morgan stiffened at the sound of Derik's voice, her heart skipping a beat. She didn't have the energy for another confrontation with him, not now. But there he was, striding up to her with that familiar look of determination etched on his face.

"What do you want, Derik?" she asked tersely, her fingers gripping the edge of the car door as if seeking an anchor.

"I just... I wanted to see how you're holding up. This case has been rough on all of us," he said, stopping a few feet from her. He glanced around the near-empty parking lot, then back at her, his eyes filled with genuine concern.

Morgan stared at him for a moment, caught off guard by his sudden show of empathy. She considered brushing him off, but something inside her craved that connection. She sighed, her shoulders sagging as she gave in to the weariness that weighed her down.

"Joe Dancer's alibi seems to have checked out. He's not our guy," she admitted, her voice barely audible. "It feels like we're chasing ghosts."

Derik nodded, his gaze locked on hers. "I know, Morgan. But we'll find him. We always do."

"Will we?" she half-whispered, the doubt seeping into her thoughts like poison. It was getting harder to believe they'd ever catch this killer, and the thought terrified her.

"Hey," Derik said more softly, stepping closer. "We're a team, remember? We'll figure this out together."

Morgan looked at him, her resolve wavering. She wanted to trust him, to lean on him as she had in the past, but the memory of his betrayal still stung. For now, though, she allowed herself a moment of vulnerability, nodding in agreement.

"Alright," she said finally, forcing a small smile.

Derik paused, avoiding her eyes for a moment. Morgan went to go into her car when he said, "Hey, can I buy you dinner?"

Morgan froze, her hand hovering above the car door handle. She turned to face him, her eyebrows knitting together in confusion. "What? Why?"

"Because you look like you could use a break," he replied, his tone gentle.

The temptation of a meal and momentary escape from the case tugged at her, but she shook her head. "I can't, Derik. I just want some alone time right now."

Derik's face fell for a moment before hardening in frustration. "We need to talk about Thomas."

"Thomas? Why? What does he have to do with anything? Don't tell me you're jealous again."

"Seriously?" Derik asked, throwing his hands up in the air. "Morgan, come on... is this your way of getting back at me or something?"

"First of all, I never agreed to go on a date with him," Morgan retorted, anger sparking in her chest. "Secondly, it's none of your business who I spend my time with."

"Of course it's my business!" Derik shouted, taking a step forward. "You're my partner, and I care about you!"

"Really?" Morgan scoffed, shaking her head. "You didn't seem to care when you betrayed me."

"Damn it, Morgan," Derik muttered, running a hand through his hair. "You know that was a mistake. I never wanted to hurt you."

"Yet, here we are," she said, her voice cold and detached.

Derik stared at her for a moment, his jaw clenched in frustration. With a resigned sigh, he took a step back. "Fine, have your alone time. But don't say I didn't warn you about Thomas."

As Derik walked away, Morgan stood by her car, her heart thumping wildly in her chest. The mention of Thomas had thrown her off guard, but she couldn't shake the feeling that there was something she could use him for - something that would help crack the case wide open. With a deep breath, she unlocked her car door and slid into the driver's seat, her mind racing with possibilities.

As Derik disappeared into the building, Morgan let out a breath. She closed her eyes, taking deep breaths to calm her racing heart. It wasn't like her to get so worked up over an argument, but the wounds left by Derik's betrayal were still too fresh, too raw.

She couldn't help but wonder if he was right about Thomas, though. Did she really know him well enough to trust him? But then again, Derik had proven that even those closest to her could betray her. With a sigh, Morgan decided to keep both men at arm's length, focusing on the case and finding the answers she so desperately sought.

CHAPTER TWENTY ONE

The streetlight above flickered like a dying firefly, casting erratic shadows on the man's face as he leaned against the cold brick wall. From his vantage point, he could see her through the window, her back to him as she worked tirelessly at her desk. She was alone in the dimly lit room, her silhouette framed by the pale glow of the computer screen.

He clenched his jaw and dug his fingers into his coat pocket, feeling the tension roll off his shoulders in waves. He didn't know her name - it didn't matter. It was the mask she wore that infuriated him, the carefully constructed persona designed to blend in with the rest of the world.

"Pathetic," he muttered under his breath, barely audible over the distant hum of city life. "Just another wolf trying to hide amongst the sheep."

His eyes narrowed, scrutinizing her every movement. Every time she smiled at her screen, he felt bile rise in his throat. The way she pretended to be so normal, so innocent, was almost enough to make him lose control right there on the street corner. But he kept himself in check, knowing that patience would yield a greater reward.

"Everyone's got a little bit of darkness inside," he whispered, his breath fogging up the window in front of him. "But some people just can't face it, can they?"

It was this hypocrisy he despised, the lies that people told themselves and others in order to survive. He'd seen it all before, but this woman - her fakery was an insult to everything he believed in. He couldn't let it stand.

"Your time will come," he promised, his voice barely audible over the wind's icy whispers. "And when it does, I'll be there to watch you crumble."

For now, he would wait, watching from the shadows as the nameless woman continued her charade. But the darkness inside him stirred, restless and insatiable, and he knew it wouldn't be long before it found its next target.

The streetlights cast a flickering glow on the wet pavement, casting shadows that danced with every gust of wind. He watched her through the window, fingers tapping impatiently on his thigh as he imagined the look of terror in her eyes when she finally realized the truth. The thought brought him an odd satisfaction, a twisted sense of justice.

"Can't wait to see your perfect little world shatter," he muttered under his breath, his voice barely audible above the distant hum of traffic. He could almost hear the sound of her heart pounding in fear, the sweet taste of panic filling the air.

The phone in his pocket vibrated suddenly, causing him to flinch. He glanced down, reading the message from an unknown number: "Are you ready?" A smirk spread across his face as he typed back, "Always."

He shifted his weight from one foot to another, the dampness seeping through the soles of his boots. The air was thick with the scent of rain and exhaust fumes, a suffocating reminder of the city's corruption. As the minutes ticked by, the anticipation swelled within him, threatening to burst free. He couldn't help but feel a thrill at the prospect of exposing her lies, her deceit.

"Tonight, everything changes," he vowed to himself, his voice low and unwavering. "No more hiding behind that mask of yours, sweetheart."

As the clock struck midnight, he saw her stand up from her desk, collect her belongings, and disappear into the back room. His heart raced with anticipation, knowing that her shift was over.

"Showtime," he whispered, stepping out of the shadows and crossing the street. He reminded himself to stay calm, to keep his emotions in check. After all, there was no turning back now. Tonight, he would put an end to her facade, and whatever twisted future she had planned for herself would be extinguished by his hand.

"Goodbye, my dear," he said softly as he approached the building, a predatory gleam in his eyes. "Your charade ends tonight."

CHAPTER TWENTY TWO

Morgan slammed the door shut behind her, her frustration echoing off the walls of her small home. Skunk, her loyal Pitbull, bounded toward her, his tail wagging excitedly as he sensed her arrival. She ruffled his fur affectionately, trying to force a smile.

"Hey, buddy," she murmured, tossing her keys onto the table by the door. But even Skunk's presence couldn't shake the weight of the argument with Derik from her mind. Why did he care so much? Was it merely jealousy, or was there something more?

"Persistent bastard," she muttered under her breath as she moved through the living room, Skunk trailing behind her.

She glanced around the familiar space, noting the cold coffee cup on the table and the stacks of case files covering every available surface. Morgan sighed, realizing that there was still no progress in the case. It felt like she was running on a treadmill – expending all her energy but getting nowhere. And she needed to eat something.

Skunk's big brown eyes followed Morgan as she paced the living room. The frustration of her unresolved argument with Derik was still weighing on her, and she couldn't shake off the feeling that he was keeping something important from her, which would be nothing new. As she continued to pace, Skunk let out a small whine of concern.

Morgan weighed her options. She needed to keep working the case, but she also needed to break for dinner, and she also wanted some damn answers on all the things Derik had been hiding from her. The men who framed her… she knew Derik would never tell.

But maybe there was someone else she could go to for help.

No, what are you thinking? she asked herself.

I could just go quickly… not too long.

Not to distract from the case.

At that moment, Morgan decided it. She couldn't focus on this weighing on her mind. She could be fast.

"Sorry, buddy," she said, pausing to give him a reassuring pat. "I'm just... I need answers."

With a sigh, Morgan flopped onto her couch and pulled out her phone. Her thumb hovered over Thomas's contact information, hesitating for a moment before tapping it. She needed help, and if Derik wasn't going to provide it, perhaps Thomas could.

Swallowing her guilt at using him, she sent him a text asking if he was free to meet up for dinner.

***

"Hi, Morgan," Thomas greeted her warmly as she entered the semi-casual restaurant, standing up from his seat at a booth near the back. His smile was genuine, but she couldn't help feeling like a fraud as she returned the gesture. There was only one reason she was here, and it wasn't to have a real date with Thomas.

"Hey, Thomas," she replied, sliding into the booth across from him. She forced herself to focus on the present, hoping that her desperation for information wouldn't be too obvious. "I actually don't have much time. I need to get back to work, but I need to eat too."

"No worries, I totally get it," Thomas said, reaching for a menu. "I figured this place would be a nice spot to keep things casual." He winked, which made Morgan's nerves rise. Thomas was a good-looking man, but this was business. Not personal. It wasn't her style to use a man's feelings for her to get closer to him or get him to do something for her, but in this case, she was sort of desperate.

Couples and families chatted happily around them, and she couldn't help but feel a pang of envy for their carefree lives.

As they perused the menu, Morgan found herself struggling to focus on the conversation. Her mind kept drifting back to the case, to Derik's possible involvement, and to her own guilt at using Thomas.

"So... where do you come from, Thomas?" Morgan asked, wanting to keep things light at first. She had to admit, she was curious about him. "I've never seen you here in Dallas before, so did you transfer?"

Thomas chuckled. "I actually grew up here in Dallas, but I left for a while and just recently came back. I've done a lot of cyber security work for more than just the FBI."

The mention of cyber security reminded Morgan why she was really here. Her thoughts drifted. Could she really ask this of Thomas?

"Is everything okay?" Thomas asked, noticing her distant expression.

Morgan shook her head, trying to clear away the thoughts. "Sorry, just a lot on my mind."

"Want to talk about it?" Thomas offered, setting down his menu.

87

Morgan hesitated, but as she looked into his kind eyes, she felt some of her tension ease. She needed to get to the point--the real reason why she'd asked him to come.

Just then, the waitress trotted up, cutting Morgan off before she could ask.

"What can I get for you two?" the waitress asked, smiling warmly.

Morgan glanced at the menu, her mind still racing. She didn't even know what she wanted. She needed to focus. She decided to keep it simple. "I'll have a burger and fries, please."

"Sure thing. And for you, sir?" the waitress asked, turning to Thomas.

"I'll have the steak sandwich," Thomas said, handing back the menu.

The waitress nodded before disappearing into the kitchen.

Morgan took a deep breath, trying to steady herself. "Thomas, I need to ask you for a favor," she said, getting straight to the point.

"Anything, Morgan," Thomas replied, his eyes locking onto hers.

"Look, I can't give you all the details," Morgan began, her voice low and urgent. "But there's a database I need access to. A database containing names. Names that might help me crack a really important case wide open."

"What case?" Thomas asked cautiously. "The one we're on now?"

"No, a different one," Morgan said. "It's... personal. And I know it's a lot to ask, but I need you to trust me on this one, Thomas. I can't tell you more than that."

Thomas's expression became guarded, and Morgan could see the cogs turning in his head. She knew this was a lot to ask, and she had no idea if he would agree to it. But she had to take the risk.

"I understand that you can't give me all the details, Morgan," Thomas said carefully. "And I want to help you, I really do. But accessing a database like that could put my job at risk. And I can't just do that on a whim."

Morgan nodded, feeling the disappointment wash over her. She knew it was a long shot, but she had to try.

"I get it," she said, glancing down at her lap. "I'm sorry for even asking."

Thomas reached out and touched her hand gently. Morgan's instincts told her to pull away, but for some reason, she stayed, allowing his fingertips to graze her skin. "But... I want to help you. I know we only just met, but..." He pulled away. "It sounds like you're asking me to do something illegal."

Morgan's heart sank. She knew it was a long shot, but she had hoped that Thomas would be willing to help her. She couldn't blame him for being cautious, though. He was a good guy, and he didn't want to get involved in anything that could harm his reputation.

"I know it's a lot to ask," Morgan said, her voice barely above a whisper. "But I'm running out of options here. I can't do this alone, and I don't know who else to turn to. I wouldn't ask a virtual stranger if it wasn't important. I'm sure you know that."

Thomas studied her for a moment, his expression softening. "Okay," he finally said. "I'll see what I can do. But you're going to have to give me something to go on. I need to know more about what you're looking for."

Morgan felt a wave of relief wash over her. She knew she was taking a risk by involving Thomas, but she didn't have any other choice. "Thank you," she said, her voice shaking slightly. "I just need names. I can send you more details."

Thomas nodded, his eyes flickering with a mixture of curiosity and concern. "Okay, but you have to promise me that this isn't going to come back and bite me, or the Bureau, in the ass. And I'm going to need some assurances that what you're doing is legal."

"I promise," Morgan said, feeling a glimmer of hope. "And I'll make sure everything is legal. I just need a way in."

Thomas leaned back in the booth, his eyes never leaving hers. "Okay, I'll do what I can." He smiled. "But you're going to owe me after this. Another date. A real one this time."

Morgan smiled, only a little. She lifted her glass. "I can agree to those terms."

CHAPTER TWENTY THREE

Carissa's knuckles whitened as she gripped the steering wheel, her heart pounding in her chest. The man beside her, the unwanted passenger who had appeared in her car as if he were a ghost materializing from the darkness, stared straight ahead, his jaw tight.

"Drive," he had commanded, and Carissa had obeyed, too terrified to do anything else. The night outside was pitch black, broken only by the headlights of her car illuminating the empty road before them. She glanced at him from the corner of her eye, trying to make out his features, but all she could see was the faint outline of his face, hardened like stone.

"Turn left up here," he ordered, his voice cold and emotionless. Carissa could barely breathe, each inhalation feeling like shards of ice piercing her lungs.

"Who are you?" she dared to whisper, her voice trembling.

"Someone who knows what you and your boss are planning," he replied, his eyes never leaving the road. "You think you can just run away with my wife's money and disappear? I won't let that happen."

A shiver ran down Carissa's spine as she realized the gravity of her situation. This man knew about their plan, about the stolen cash and the plan to leave town for good. How could he have found out? Who could have told him?

"Listen," she stammered, struggling to find the right words, "I don't know what you're talking about."

"Save it," he cut her off, staring intently into the shadows of the night. "I know everything. I've been watching you, and I've seen how you and your boss work together, laughing and flirting behind the bar. You thought no one noticed, didn't you?"

Carissa's cheeks burned with shame, her insides twisting with fear. He had been watching her, and she hadn't had the slightest clue. She felt exposed, vulnerable, as if she were a helpless prey cornered by a ruthless predator.

"Please," she begged, "I don't want any trouble. I'll give you the money back, just let me go."

He turned to face her for the first time, his eyes locking onto hers with an intensity that made her flinch. "You think it's that simple?" he hissed. "You've already crossed a line, and there's no going back."

Carissa's hands trembled on the wheel, her thoughts racing as fast as her heart. Her breathing grew shallow, each inhale a desperate gasp for air. She needed to come up with a plan, a way to escape this nightmare.

"Think, Carissa, think," she chided herself, forcing her eyes to focus on the road.

"Nice night, isn't it?" he said suddenly, his voice calm, almost jovial. It caught her off guard.

"Y-yeah, I guess so," she stuttered, unsure how to respond. Was he trying to put her at ease, or was this just another twisted game of his?

"Look, I don't want any trouble either," he continued, his tone softening. "But you have to understand my position."

"Your position?" she scoffed, anger momentarily overpowering her fear. "You're the one who kidnapped me! This is all your fault!"

"Is it?" he countered, raising an eyebrow. "Or is it yours for getting involved in something that doesn't concern you?"

The words stung, and Carissa found herself blinking back tears. She couldn't let him see her cry; she had to stay strong. But as the silence stretched between them, she felt the heat rising in her cheeks, sweat breaking out across her forehead.

"Are you okay?" he asked, genuine concern coloring his voice. "You don't look so good."

"Of course I'm not okay!" she snapped, her pulse pounding in her ears. "I've been kidnapped by a lunatic, and I have no idea if I'll ever make it home again!"

"Alright, alright," he relented, holding up his hands in surrender. "Pull over. Let me out."

"Really?" she asked skeptically, her heart leaping at the prospect of freedom. But as she steered the car onto the shoulder, doubt crept in. Was he going to let her go, or was this just another trap? She couldn't be sure, and that uncertainty gnawed at her gut like a hungry beast.

"Go on, pull over," he urged, his voice gentle, almost soothing. "I promise, I'm not going to hurt you."

She hesitated for a moment longer before acquiescing, pressing down on the brake and bringing the car to a stop. As she shifted into park, her chest tightened with anxiety, nausea roiling in her stomach.

Whether he meant to hurt her or not, Carissa couldn't shake the feeling that her ordeal was far from over.

The door creaked open, and the kidnapper stepped out, lingering for a moment before closing it again. He flashed Carissa a tight-lipped smile, as if to reassure her one last time that he meant no harm.

"Take care of yourself," he said softly before turning away.

Heart pounding, she barely allowed him to take a step away from the car before she slammed her foot on the gas pedal, sending gravel flying in all directions. She didn't dare look back, focusing solely on putting as much distance between them as possible.

"Finally," she whispered to herself, trying to calm her racing heart. "I'm free."

Her hands tightened around the steering wheel, slick with sweat inside the gloves he'd given her earlier. They were black leather, an odd gift from a man who had terrified her only moments ago. The uneasiness in her stomach grew stronger, making it difficult to focus on the road ahead.

"Stay calm," she told herself, taking deep breaths to steady her nerves. "Just get home and forget about this nightmare."

As she rounded a bend, the headlights of an oncoming vehicle pierced the darkness, momentarily blinding her. She squinted, struggling to see past the sudden glare, but her vision blurred, and her head swam with dizziness. Panic gripped her as her body betrayed her, her limbs growing heavy and unresponsive.

What's happening to me? she thought frantically, her breathing shallow and labored. *Am I having a heart attack? A stroke?*

The car veered toward the center line as her grip on the steering wheel slackened, the cold reality of her situation settling in like a shroud. The oncoming headlights drew closer, their blinding light the last thing she saw as the world went dark around her.

CHAPTER TWENTY FOUR

The first rays of sunlight seeped through the blinds, casting thin strips of light onto Morgan's face. She groaned and pulled the covers over her head, trying to ignore the persistent headache that throbbed behind her eyes. Her mouth was dry, as if she'd been chewing on cotton balls all night. Damn whiskey, she thought.

She knew she shouldn't have had that last drink, but the memories of yesterday weighed heavily on her conscience. In a moment of desperation, she had asked Thomas for help – something she rarely did. He was brilliant with computers, and she had needed his expertise to dig deeper into the database that held vital information about the case.

Morgan couldn't shake the guilt of involving Thomas in her personal crusade for justice. He was a good guy, but she had dragged him into a dangerous game. What if someone found out he had helped her? He could lose everything: his job, his freedom, maybe even his life. It was a risk she had been willing to take for herself, but putting Thomas in the line of fire made her stomach churn.

"God, what have I done?" she whispered, rubbing her temples.

As she lay there, the room slowly brightened, and she knew she couldn't hide from the day any longer. With a sigh, she swung her legs over the side of the bed and planted her feet on the cold hardwood floor. The chill sent shivers up her spine, but it also cleared some of the cobwebs from her mind.

Morgan stood and stretched her aching limbs, feeling the stiffness in her muscles from another restless night. She glanced at the clock on the wall: 6:15 AM. It was a new day, and despite her guilt and the lingering effects of her hangover, she had work to do. There was still a killer on the loose, and she couldn't afford to waste any more time.

The hard edges of determination forged by years of adversity settled over Morgan like a suit of armor, pushing the guilt and uncertainty to the back of her mind. There would be time for second-guessing later; right now, she had work to do. She pulled on a pair of dark jeans and a gray button-down shirt, her movements swift and efficient. The familiar weight of her gun holstered at her side was both a comfort and a reminder of the stakes.

Her fingers were just finishing with the last button when her phone rang, the pulsating tone slicing through the early morning quiet. Without hesitation, she grabbed it and pressed it to her ear. "Cross."

"Hey, Morgan, it's Derik," said the voice on the other end. There was an undercurrent of urgency in his tone that instantly set her on edge. "We've got another one."

"Where?" Her heart thundered in her chest, adrenaline flooding her system as the weariness of the hangover receded.

"Car crash near Pine Street, on the outskirts of town. Looks like the same M.O. as the others." Derik's words were clipped, professional, but she could hear the concern beneath them. They'd been tracking this killer for months, and each new victim only heightened their sense of helplessness.

"Damn it," Morgan muttered, clenching her free hand into a fist. Another life was taken, and another family was left shattered. And still no closer to catching the bastard responsible. "I'll be there ASAP."

"Be careful, Morgan. We don't know what we're dealing with yet." Derik's warning was unnecessary – she knew all too well the dangers they faced – but she appreciated it all the same. It was good to know someone had her back.

"Always am," she replied, her voice steady, despite her anxious thoughts. She ended the call and took a deep breath, her eyes flicking to the small framed photo on the bedside table: a younger version of herself, smiling and carefree. A lifetime ago.

"Let's catch this son of a bitch," she whispered, and strode out of the room, her resolve hardening with each step.

***

The sun was a pale disc in the sky, casting weak light on the quiet street as Morgan pulled up to the scene. Her heart hammered against her ribcage; she knew what awaited her, but it didn't make it any easier to face. She stepped out of her car, gravel crunching beneath her boots, and took a moment to steady herself before approaching the wreckage.

"Hey, Morgan," Derik greeted her grimly as she hurried over, flashing lights casting eerie shadows across his face. "I wish we were meeting under better circumstances."

In truth, Morgan wished they weren't meeting at all. It bothered her how Derik could act so casually with her after everything that had happened. He had betrayed her in numerous ways, lying to her about his knowledge about the people who framed her, for one, and two, the fact that he still hadn't told her what she needed to know. Morgan had accepted that maybe Derik had just been a pawn to those men too, that maybe he did know nothing…

But it didn't mean she had to trust him.

Still, when she looked at his face, she couldn't help but feel a tug of familiarity. His sharp green eyes, his black hair slicked back the way it usually was, but messier than he used to hold it. The stress was evident on his face, but still, he was as handsome as he always had been. Morgan slapped herself for even thinking about it.

She had to remind herself of who he was now… the same guy who desperately stopped her car on the highway not long ago to stop her from driving into a trap, a trap he'd set. He got points for stopping it, of course, but Morgan wasn't about to open back up.

Instead, she kept things casual so she could focus on her job:

"It is what it is, Greene," she replied, her voice tight with frustration. "What do we have?"

"Car crash," he said, gesturing towards the mangled vehicle wrapped around a pole. "But the victim… well, you should see for yourself."

Morgan steeled herself and peered through the shattered window. A woman, no older than thirty-five, sat slumped in the driver's seat. Her eyes were glassy and unseeing, her mouth twisted in a final expression of terror. But it was her hands that caught Morgan's attention – gloved and glued to the steering wheel, just like the others.

"Jesus," she breathed, feeling a wave of nausea rise in her throat. This was the fourth victim in as many weeks, and the pattern was unmistakable. "It's definitely him, isn't it?"

"Seems likely," agreed Derik, his brow furrowed in concern. "We won't know for sure until forensics has had a proper look, but I'd bet my badge on it."

"Dammit." Morgan clenched her fists, her nails biting into her palms. The killer was escalating, growing bolder with each attack. How many more lives would be lost before they could stop him?

"Hey," Derik said gently, touching her arm. "We're going to catch this guy, Morgan. I promise."

"Are we?" she asked, her voice thick with doubt. "Because it feels like we're always one step behind."

"Maybe," he admitted. "But we've got a good team working on this. And we've got you – the best damn agent I know."

"Flattery won't solve this case, Derik." Despite herself, she felt a small smile tug at the corner of her lips. It was nice to know he believed in her, even if she didn't always believe in herself.

"Maybe not," he conceded, returning her smile. "But it might just help keep us going until we do."

Morgan took a deep breath, forcing herself to focus on the task at hand. "Alright," she said, determination settling over her like armor. "We have an ID yet?"

"Clarissa Watkins," Derik said, breaking the silence as he read from a small notebook. "Thirty-two years old. This is her car."

Morgan glanced at him, taking in the grim expression on his face. "What happened to her?"

"According to the coroner's preliminary report, she was dead before the impact with the pole." Derik closed the notebook and pocketed it. "Looks like our killer struck again."

Morgan felt a chill run down her spine. She eyed the gloves on Clarissa's hands, the way they seemed unnaturally fused to the steering wheel. "Make sure forensics tests those gloves," she instructed Derik. "If this is the work of the same killer, then the poison in the gloves is what did her in, just like the others."

"Right away." Derik nodded, motioning for a nearby officer to alert the forensics team.

Morgan studied the scene in front of her, looking for any sign that could lead them closer to the person responsible for these heinous acts. Her mind raced as she tried to piece together the victim's final moments.

Morgan took a step back, feeling woozy. The hangover from the night before was still wreaking havoc on her system. She blinked against the intrusive sunlight filtering through the trees, and that's when she saw him.

Down the street from where Clarissa Watkins' car was parked, there was a bar with chipped paint and a neon sign flickering in the morning light. Standing outside the entrance, barely visible against the shadows cast by the old brick building, was a man. He appeared to be watching the crime scene from afar, his features too indistinct to make out any details. But something about his form was familiar.

"Derik," she called quietly, her gaze locked on the distant figure. "Do you see that guy down by the bar?"

Derik squinted in the direction she indicated. "Yeah, I see him. Why?"

"I can't shake this feeling..." Morgan trailed off, her mind racing. This wasn't the first time she'd felt like someone was watching her at a crime scene. It was as if they were always one step ahead, lurking in the shadows just beyond her grasp.

"Feeling?" Derik prompted, his eyes narrowing in concern.

"Like we're being watched," she admitted, the words tasting bitter on her tongue. "Every crime scene we've been at, I can't help but feel like there's someone observing us."

"Could be a coincidence," Derik offered. "You know how things are, people always want to get a look at a crime scene."

But when Morgan looked back, the man was gone. Maybe he went inside the bar, or maybe he just disappeared.

Morgan's heart raced as she scanned the area, trying to catch a glimpse of the man again. She knew it couldn't be a coincidence, not anymore. Too many things were adding up, too many clues pointing towards someone with inside information.

"I'm gonna go see if he's in the bar," she said, her voice low and urgent. "You stay here."

"You sure? I can come with."

"No," Morgan said, "it's probably nothing. Just make sure we cover all our bases here."

"Roger that. Be careful."

Morgan nodded, turning her gaze toward the bar. Without a second thought, she took off up the street.

CHAPTER TWENTY FIVE

Determined to pursue her gut feeling, Morgan strode toward the bar. With each step, her hangover seemed to fade, replaced by a steely resolve. This was the moment – the one that would either confirm her suspicions or finally put them to rest.

The bar's door creaked as it swung open, revealing a dimly-lit dive with the unmistakable scent of stale beer and cigarette smoke. A handful of patrons nursed their morning drinks at the counter, heads buried in plates of greasy breakfast food. Behind the bar, a grizzled bartender wiped down glasses with a stained cloth, his eyes watchful beneath a furrowed brow.

"Excuse me," Morgan said, catching the bartender's attention. "I need to ask you about someone."

"Who might that be?" The barman replied, setting down the glass he was cleaning.

"Someone was watching from outside just now," Morgan explained, her voice steady despite the unease she felt. "A man, but I didn't get a good look at him. Did you see him?"

"Can't say I did," he responded, shaking his head. "Lots of people come and go around here."

Morgan bit back her frustration. She knew he was hiding something. But how could she prove it? She glanced around the room, searching for any clue – any sign at all – that might help her understand the connection between the man outside and this grimy bar.

"Look," she said, leaning in closer to the bartender. "I'm an FBI agent investigating a series of murders. If you know anything, I need you to tell me."

The bartender hesitated, his gaze shifting nervously between Morgan and the other patrons. Finally, he sighed. "Look, I didn't see anyone," he said. "And no one's walked in here in thirty minutes, so I don't think the guy you're looking for is one of my regulars."

Damn. Morgan bit her lip, disappointed. She glanced around the bar. It was early, but even now, people were drinking. She saw a man spilling his guts to another man over a beer.

"And yeah, I did cheat on my wife, but she deserved it, didn't she?" he said.

"You should probably keep that to yourself, man," another man said back.

He was right. Drunk people often spilled their secrets.

Secrets...

Each one of the victims had a darker secret. Morgan had been stumped, trying to figure out how the killer could have been finding them out.

But maybe...

Maybe he did it by hanging around a place like this.

It was probably a shot in the dark, but Morgan had to try.

Morgan's heart raced as she dug through her pockets, pulling out a stack of photographs she'd taken from the case files. She couldn't shake the feeling that there was a connection between the man who had been watching and this bar.

"Can I ask you something else?" she inquired, holding up the photos like a deck of cards. "Have you seen any of these people before?"

The bartender eyed the images warily, taking one from her hand and studying it for a moment. Morgan could see the gears turning in his head, the faintest flicker of recognition dancing in his eyes.

"Actually, yeah," he admitted, pointing to a photo of a red-haired woman with a bright smile. "She used to come in here all the time. Always sat at the end of the bar, near the door. Ordered the same thing every week: a cheeseburger with extra pickles, and a rum and Coke."

Morgan felt a chill run down her spine as she studied the woman's face, wondering what had brought her into the killer's crosshairs.

"Any of the others?" she pressed, handing him the next photograph.

"Uh, yeah," he said, nodding slowly as he gazed at an image of Amy Sanderson. "She was in here a few times too. She mostly talked about herself, got really drunk, and bought a lot of drinks. I had to cut her off."

"Anyone else?" Morgan asked, her voice barely more than a whisper now as she handed him another photo – this one of a young woman with dark hair and a shy smile.

"Her too," he replied, hesitating for a moment before continuing. "She didn't say much, at least not till you got a few drinks in her. Then she was an open faucet."

As the bartender continued to recognize each of the victims, Morgan's heart pounded in her chest. The connection between the bar and the murders was stronger than she'd anticipated, and it filled her with a renewed sense of urgency.

Morgan looked around the dimly lit bar, taking in the cracked leather stools and neon beer signs that cast a hazy glow over the room. She could almost taste the desperation clinging to the air, heavy with the scent of stale alcohol and cigarette smoke. It was exactly the kind of place where people came to forget their troubles, to pour out their souls.

"By the way," Morgan said, her voice steady despite the pounding in her chest, "what's your name?"

The bartender wiped down the counter with an old rag before answering, "Davis Smith."

"Nice to meet you, Davis," she replied.

"Likewise," Davis responded, nodding. He leaned against the bar, his hands gripping the edge as he spoke. "You know, people come in here all the time, have a couple of drinks, and start talking. Sometimes they tell me things – personal stuff. It's part of the job, I guess. Just listening."

Morgan studied Davis's face, trying to discern if there was something he wasn't telling her. With every victim having been in this bar at some point, it seemed unlikely that he wouldn't have heard anything that could be relevant. But she couldn't force him to talk – she needed him to trust her.

For all she knew, Davis could be their killer.

"Is there anything you've heard recently that might help me?" she asked carefully, her eyes never leaving his. "Anything unusual or out of the ordinary?"

Davis rubbed his chin thoughtfully, his eyes narrowing as he considered her question. "There's always something unusual going on in a dive like this," he muttered, chuckling dryly. "But I haven't noticed anything particularly strange lately. At least, nothing I can put my finger on."

Morgan's mind raced, her instincts telling her that Davis knew more than he was letting on. She took a deep breath, trying to calm herself and formulate a plan. If she wanted to get the information she needed, she would have to play this smart – and patient.

"Can I see a list of your staff, Davis?" Morgan asked, her eyes scanning the dimly lit room for any clues that might help her case. The smell of stale beer and cigarette smoke clung to the air, making her feel even more on edge.

"List?" Davis chuckled, the sound echoing through the empty bar. "It's just me, sweetheart. Well, it was just me and a barback, but he up and vanished a few days ago. No notice, nothing. Left me in the lurch."

"Really?" Morgan said, an icy chill running down her spine as she considered the implications. A sudden disappearance so close to a murder scene couldn't be coincidental. "What did this barback look like?"

"Ah, I dunno. Average height, brown hair, kinda scruffy-looking," Davis replied, shrugging his shoulders.

Morgan's gaze drifted over to a Christmas photo hanging on the wall, the cheerful faces of the bar's patrons contrasting sharply with the grim reality outside.

Among them, a young man in a uniform stood out, a pair of gloves on his hands. Her heart tightened in her chest as she recognized him instantly.

"Wait a minute…" Morgan breathed, her voice barely a whisper. She moved closer to the photograph, feeling a cold sweat break out on her brow. It was him.

Joe Dancer.

"Is that your barback?" she asked, pointing at the man in the photo. Her mind raced, her thoughts a jumbled mess of fear, anger, and regret. How could she have been so blind?

Davis squinted at the photo, then nodded slowly. "Yeah, that's him. John, or whatever his name is."

"Joe Dancer," Morgan said.

"That's it," Davis replied. "You know him?"

Morgan clenched her fists, the weight of guilt bearing down on her like a thousand-pound anvil. She had been so close – so close to cracking this case wide open, and she hadn't even realized it. But now she knew, and there was no turning back.

"Thanks, Davis," she said, her voice firm and resolute. "You've been more helpful than you know." As she turned to leave the bar, a fire burned within her, fueled by both her desire for justice and her need to right a wrong that had haunted her for far too long. This time, she would catch the killer – no matter what the cost.

CHAPTER TWENTY SIX

The man's heart pounded in his chest as he sprinted down the busy Dallas street, weaving through the swarm of pedestrians like a snake through tall grass. Sweat poured down his face and his breath came in ragged gasps, but he couldn't slow down – not now. She was leaving tonight, sooner than he'd expected. He had to get her today.

"Excuse me! Sorry!" he panted, shoving past a couple who glared at him in annoyance. He didn't have time for their judgment. The weight of his mission bore down on him like an iron anchor, dragging him forward with an urgency that left no room for social niceties.

"Liars and cheats," he muttered under his breath, the words coming out as little more than a growl. "Fake narcissists, all of them."

It wasn't just her; it was everyone. The whole city seemed to be crawling with people living double lives, pretending to be something they weren't. It made him sick. But he couldn't think about that now; he needed to focus on his target.

"Watch it, buddy!" snapped a man in a suit as the two collided, jostling each other off balance for a moment. The man barely registered the encounter, already scanning the street ahead for any sign of her workplace.

"Almost there," he told himself, gritting his teeth and pushing his body harder. He could feel the strain in his muscles, the burn that threatened to overwhelm him, but he refused to let it slow him down.

"Can't stand liars," he thought again, repeating the mantra that had kept him going all these years. "People who live double lives...I'm not like them."

He knew he was different, honest, and true in a way that so few people ever were. He would see this through to the end, no matter what it took. And as he finally rounded the corner and spotted the cafe where she worked, his resolve hardened even further. She would not escape him. She would pay for her lies and deceit, just like all the others had.

"Today," he promised himself, eyes locked on the waitress through the window. "I'll get her today."

The sweltering Dallas sun beat down on his back as he navigated the crowded sidewalk, but he could barely feel it through the thin fabric of his gloves. He wished he didn't have to wear them, but it was a necessity; his skin couldn't handle direct sunlight for long periods without becoming unbearably painful.

"Excuse me," he muttered, sidestepping around a woman pushing a stroller. The gloves made him stand out in the heat, but he couldn't go without them. It wasn't like he was hiding anything, he told himself. It was simply a matter of self-preservation.

"Hey, you dropped your wallet!" called a passerby, waving the black leather billfold in the air.

"Thanks," he said, snatching it from the stranger's grasp and continuing on his way. His heart pounded in his chest, threatening to burst free at any moment. He couldn't afford any more delays – she might leave before he got there.

"Stupid condition," he thought, cursing his luck. If it weren't for the sensitivity of his skin, he wouldn't need these gloves or any of the other precautions that slowed him down, that made him conspicuous. But there was no use dwelling on it. He was born this way, and there was nothing he could do to change it.

As he finally arrived at the cafe, he took a deep breath and tried to steady his racing thoughts. This was it. The moment he'd been waiting for, planning for, for weeks. He could see her through the window, chatting with customers, completely unaware of what was coming.

"Liars, cheats, all of them," he muttered under his breath as he slowed to a stop outside the cafe. He wiped the sweat from his brow with the back of his gloved hand and steadied himself against the brick wall, his chest heaving. "But not me. I'm the real deal."

Through the window, he spotted her – the waitress, a woman of about twenty-five with long, dark hair and a smile that could light up a room. She was laughing, wiping down tables, and flirting with customers in equal measure. It made his stomach churn with disgust. She had no idea the life she was about to ruin when she eloped with her teacher tonight.

"Pathetic," he growled, watching her closely as she moved through the crowded dining area. "They're all living a lie, but not me. I see right through them."

"Excuse me, sir?" A voice interrupted his thoughts, causing him to flinch. It was a young woman holding a paper cup of steaming coffee. "You've been standing there for a while now. Are you waiting for someone?"

"Uh, yeah," he replied, trying to sound casual as he peeled himself away from the wall. "Just catching my breath."

"Okay, well, have a good day!" she said cheerfully, walking away with a bounce in her step.

"Damn it, focus!" he scolded himself as he watched her disappear down the street. He couldn't afford any distractions right now. He had a job to do.

"Can I help you?" The waitress' voice rang out as he pushed open the door to the cafe. Her eyes met his, and for a moment, he thought he saw a flicker of recognition before she quickly masked it with a warm smile.

"Uh, yeah, just a coffee," he stammered, trying to act normal. She nodded and reached for a cup, her fingers brushing against his as she handed it over. He tensed, but forced himself to maintain eye contact.

"Great," she said, smiling back at him. "Enjoy your coffee."

"Thanks," he replied, forcing a smile of his own. "I will."

As he sat down at a nearby table, his thoughts raced. He knew he needed to get her alone, to confront her before she had a chance to leave with her lover. But how? His eyes darted around the room, searching for inspiration.

"Sir?" The waitress was standing by his table, holding out a small plate of pastries. "Would you like one?"

He looked up at her, feigning surprise. "Oh, um, sure," he said, reaching for a croissant. "Thanks."

"No problem," she replied, flashing that disarming grin again. "Let me know if you need anything else."

"Actually, there is something," he said, seizing the opportunity. "Could I talk to you outside for a moment? It's important."

"Uh, sure," she answered hesitantly, casting a wary glance at her manager. "Just give me a second."

"Take your time," he assured her, trying to keep his voice steady. "I'll be right outside."

His heart pounded in his chest as he waited for her, his gloved hands gripping the edge of the table. This was it. There was no turning back now. He just hoped that, once it was all over, he could finally convince himself that he wasn't living a lie – that he was doing what was necessary to expose the dishonesty of others.

"Okay, I'm here," the waitress said, stepping outside and closing the door behind her. "What did you want to talk about?"

"Your plans tonight," he replied, his voice cold and steady. "I know what you're planning to do, and I'm here to stop you."

"Wh-what are you talking about?" she stammered, her eyes wide with fear.

"Your elopement," he said bluntly. "It ends now."

CHAPTER TWENTY SEVEN

Morgan's knuckles turned white as she gripped the steering wheel, weaving through Dallas traffic with a determination that left other drivers honking in her wake. The sun glared down on her, but she paid it no mind; all she could think about was getting to Joe Dancer's house before it was too late.

"Dammit," she muttered under her breath, cursing herself for letting Joe go earlier. She had believed his alibi, that he had been playing piano at the time of the murder. But now, knowing he had been in the neighborhood where one of the victims had been killed, she couldn't ignore the nagging feeling that they had let their suspect slip right through their fingers.

"Focus, Morgan, focus," she told herself, eyes darting between the road and the GPS device on her dashboard. Her heart raced, remembering the weight of the prison jumpsuit she'd worn for ten years after being framed for murder. She'd become too complacent, too distracted by thoughts of those who had betrayed her when she should have been zeroing in on this case.

As she sped past another car, narrowly avoiding a collision, Morgan's mind raced with thoughts of Joe – how he played the piano so beautifully, how he had seemed so innocent. She shook her head, trying to clear it of doubts. If there was even a chance he was their killer, she had to act fast.

"Come on, come on," she urged herself, pressing harder on the gas pedal. The cityscape blurred past her, a whirlwind of colors and shapes that barely registered in her peripheral vision.

Joe Dancer, you better be home. She growled, teeth grinding together as she imagined him slipping away once more. But she refused to let that happen. Not again. Never again would she allow someone to escape justice because of her own mistakes.

As she closed in on Joe's house, Morgan took a deep breath, steeling herself for what she might find. There was no turning back now – it was time to face the truth and bring this killer to justice once and for all.

No more fuck-ups, no more distractions. The sirens of the cop cars behind her grew louder, reminding her that she wasn't alone in this pursuit. She had to focus on the task at hand - finding Joe Dancer and bringing him to justice.

Glancing at the rearview mirror, she saw the flashing lights of her backup, a fleet of police cruisers swerving through traffic, determined to keep pace with her. She couldn't help but feel a sense of reassurance knowing they were there, ready to support her when the time came.

"Cross, any updates?" crackled the voice of Derik over the radio.

"Nothing yet," she replied tersely, her eyes scanning the road ahead for any sign of Joe's house. "I'll let you know when I get there."

As she continued driving, Morgan couldn't shake the feeling that she was missing something crucial about the case. Suddenly, the pieces clicked into place in her mind, and she realized how Joe had been killing these women. He must have been listening to their darkest secrets while working at the bar, using the information to blackmail them. And all he asked in return was for them to wear those damn gloves.

"Derik," she said urgently into the radio, "I think I know how Joe's doing it. He's blackmailing these women, forcing them to wear the gloves."

"Blackmail? For what purpose? To make them suffer?" Derik's voice conveyed his confusion.

"Maybe," Morgan mused, her thoughts racing. "Or maybe it's about control. By making them wear the gloves, he knows their deepest secrets are safe with him."

"But why kill them?"

"Perhaps it's his twisted sense of justice," Morgan offered. "He believes he's ridding the world of 'fakes' - people who hide their true selves."

"Jesus," Derik muttered. "We need to find him, now."

"Agreed," Morgan said, her resolve hardening. This was it - the moment she had been working towards since returning to the FBI. She would not let this killer slip through her fingers again.

With renewed determination, Morgan pressed down on the accelerator, the powerful engine roaring beneath her as she sped towards Joe Dancer's house, ready to confront the man behind the gloves and put an end to his reign of terror.

Morgan's heart pounded in her chest as she swerved through the Dallas streets, the flashing lights of the squad cars reflecting off the glass buildings around her. The gravity of the situation weighed on her like a lead vest, her mind racing with the horrifying details of Joe Dancer's sick and twisted methods. The poison he had concocted for those gloves was slow-acting but lethal, giving his victims just enough time to fully comprehend the consequences of their darkest secrets before succumbing to their fate.

As she skidded to a halt in front of Joe's house, Morgan knew she couldn't waste another second. She flung open the car door, her FBI badge glinting in the sunlight, and sprinted towards the unassuming residence. Banging her fist against the wooden door, she yelled, "FBI! Open up!"

"Joe Dancer, we know you're in there!" she added, attempting to sound more confident than she felt. But the silence that greeted her only fueled her growing sense of dread. What if he wasn't here? What if he was already out there, targeting another victim?

"Damn it," she muttered under her breath, her mind racing with possibilities. Was she too late? Had Joe slipped through her fingers again? She couldn't allow herself to dwell on the past mistakes, not now.

"Maybe he's hiding inside," she thought, trying to maintain her focus. But as she stood outside the silent house, an eerie feeling crept over her; something was amiss.

"Joe, I swear, if you don't come out right now, I'll break this door down myself!" Morgan threatened, knowing that time was of the essence. But still, no response came. Her pulse quickened, adrenaline coursing through her veins like fire. Every second that ticked by was another second closer to another life ruined, another family torn apart by this monster.

"Alright, you asked for it," she said, stepping back and preparing to kick down the door. As her foot connected with the sturdy wood, splinters flying and the door crashing open, Morgan knew that she couldn't afford any more mistakes.

"Joe Dancer!" she shouted, gun drawn as she entered the eerily quiet house. "You can't hide from me anymore!"

But as she searched the tidy rooms, her determination began to wane. Where was he? Was she too late? Or had she simply been wrong about Joe all along?

Morgan's heart pounded as the sound of sirens approached, her breaths coming in short, shallow bursts. She glanced over her shoulder to see several police cars pulling up at a breakneck pace, tires screeching as they came to a halt. Derik emerged from one of the vehicles, his face a mixture of worry and determination.

"About time you got here," Morgan said through gritted teeth. "I need you to break into this house. Now!"

"Roger that!" Derik replied, motioning for the other officers to follow him as they made their way to the door. The air was thick with tension, each officer fully aware of the stakes at hand.

"Ready?" Derik asked, looking at Morgan for confirmation.

"Stay sharp," she whispered, her voice barely audible over the pounding of her own heartbeat. The team moved cautiously through the house, the only sounds their synchronized footsteps and the occasional creak of floorboards beneath them.

"Clear!" one officer called out from a nearby room, followed by similar affirmations from others as they searched. As Morgan stepped further into the living room, she couldn't help but notice the unsettling tidiness of the space. Every piece of furniture was precisely placed, every surface spotless, as if someone had meticulously arranged everything within an inch of its life. It was almost too perfect, too controlled—like a reflection of the twisted mind they were hunting.

"Derik," she whispered, her voice tense with unease. "This place...it's too clean. Something's not right."

"Be on your guard," he cautioned, his eyes narrowing as he took in the unnerving scene before them. "Joe could be hiding anywhere."

"Or waiting for us," she added, her thoughts racing with possible scenarios.

"Stay focused, Morgan," Derik urged, his voice a steadying presence amidst the chaos of her mind. "We'll find him and put an end to this."

"Right," Morgan agreed, taking a deep breath as she pushed away her doubts. She couldn't afford any more mistakes; too many lives were at stake. Joe Dancer had evaded her grasp for too long, but not anymore. Today, it would all come to an end.

"Let's keep moving," she said, firm resolve in her voice as she led the team deeper into the house.

***

The sickly sweet scent of chemicals hung heavy in the air as Morgan and her team split up, methodically combing through Joe's house. Room by room, they found nothing but an eerie emptiness, a void where the man they were hunting should have been.

"Basement's clear," called out Officer Martinez, his voice echoing through the otherwise hushed space. "Just some storage down there."

"Keep looking," Morgan ordered, unwilling to accept that Joe had slipped through their fingers once more. She couldn't shake the nagging feeling that they were missing something crucial, that the key to unraveling this twisted web lay just out of reach.

As the others continued their search, Morgan descended into the basement, her flashlight beam slicing through the gloom. She couldn't let it go; she needed to see for herself. She knew Joe too well at this point—every dark corner of his mind, every hidden secret. He was here, somewhere, lurking just beneath the surface.

"Come on, you son of a bitch," she muttered under her breath, scanning the cluttered space with renewed determination. Boxes and old furniture formed a maze-like network around her, each shadow harboring the potential for danger.

"Something's not right," she whispered, pausing mid-step as the familiar scent of chemicals intensified. Her pulse quickened, adrenaline surging through her veins as she realized what lay before her—Joe's makeshift chemistry lab.

"Derik, get down here!" she shouted, her voice cracking with urgency. "I found it."

"Found what?" Derik asked as he appeared at the top of the stairs, concern etched on his face.

"His lab," she replied, stepping aside to reveal the grim tableau. Flasks and beakers filled with viscous liquids sat atop a stained workbench, surrounded by scribbled formulas and ominous-looking equipment. A pair of latex gloves lay discarded nearby, their insides coated with a sinister residue.

"Jesus," Derik breathed, taking in the scene with a mixture of horror and fascination. "This is where he made the poison."

"Exactly," Morgan confirmed, her eyes locked on the gloves. Each one was a deadly instrument, capable of inflicting unimaginable pain and suffering. And they had Joe's fingerprints all over them. "We've got him now."

"Or he's got us right where he wants us," Derik countered, his voice tight with apprehension. He knew, as well as she did, that this was far from over.

"Either way," Morgan said, her gaze never leaving the gloves, "we're not giving up until we find him. No more mistakes. No more victims."

"Agreed," Derik replied, his resolve matching hers. "We'll bring him to justice, Morgan. I promise you that."

As they stood there amidst the darkness and decay, united by a common goal, Morgan allowed herself a small, bitter smile. They were closer than ever to ending Joe's reign of terror, but she knew the hardest part was yet to come. The final battle still loomed before them, and she could only hope they'd be ready when it arrived.

Morgan's heart thundered in her chest as she sprinted up the basement stairs, each step echoing her mounting urgency. She burst into the living room where Derik and the rest of the team were still searching for any trace of Joe. "I found his lab," she blurted out between breaths, her voice raw with determination. "He's our killer, no doubt about it."

"Where is he now?" Derik asked, his eyes narrowing in concern.

"God knows, but we need to find him. Fast." Morgan scanned the faces of the agents surrounding her, their expressions a mix of fear, anger, and resolve. "We've got the evidence we need. Now let's finish this."

As the team dispersed, their movements swift and efficient, Morgan couldn't shake the growing sense of dread that gnawed at her insides. If they didn't find Joe soon, another innocent life would be lost. And the weight of that failure would fall squarely on her shoulders.

CHAPTER TWENTY EIGHT

Morgan's heart pounded in her chest as she pushed open the heavy doors of the dimly-lit bar. The familiar scent of stale beer and worn leather filled her nostrils, but she had no time for nostalgia. Davis, the bartender, was wiping down the counter with a damp cloth, his brow furrowed in concentration.

"Back already?" He looked up, surprise flickering across his features as he took in Morgan's tense expression. "What can I do for you, Agent Cross?"

"Think, Davis," Morgan said, her voice urgent as she leaned against the bar, her knuckles turning white from the force of her grip. "Were there any women who spilled some big secret here at the bar? Ones I didn't show you earlier?"

Davis chewed on the inside of his cheek, his eyes darting around the room as if the answer might be scrawled on the walls in invisible ink. "I, uh...I'm not sure, Agent Cross. There were a lot of people who talked to Joe. A lot of secrets."

"Please, Davis," Morgan implored, her eyes locked onto his with a fierce intensity that made him shift uncomfortably. "It's crucial we find out if there are any other potential targets. You have to remember something, anything that could help us."

"Okay, okay," Davis stammered, his hands nervously twisting the edge of the damp cloth. "I'm trying to think. Just give me a second." He closed his eyes, his brow furrowing in concentration, and Morgan could practically see the gears turning in his head, sifting through countless memories of late nights and hushed conversations.

"Take your time," Morgan whispered, her fingers tapping an impatient rhythm against the polished wood of the bar. But inside, her thoughts screamed for answers, for the key that would unlock Joe Dancer's twisted game.

Davis's eyes snapped open, and he looked at Morgan with a sudden clarity. "Wait, there was one girl. It was just before Joe quit. She was young, maybe college-aged, and she told me she was dating her teacher. She said they were planning to elope, even though he had a family and kids."

Morgan leaned in closer, her heart pounding in her chest. "Tell me everything you remember about her. We need to find her."

"Okay, okay," Davis said, his voice cracking slightly under the pressure. He rubbed his temples, trying to summon the memory. "When she came in, she was pretty upset. Kept going on about how much she loved this guy, but felt guilty because of his wife and children. I remember checking her ID when she ordered a drink – her name started with an 'M,' like Mary or Marie or something."

"Did she say anything else about her relationship with her teacher?" Morgan asked, her mind racing as she tried to piece together the puzzle.

"Uh, not much," Davis replied, racking his brain for any details that might be helpful. "She mentioned that her teacher was helping her learn something out of the ordinary for someone her age, but I don't remember what it was exactly."

"Anything, Davis. Even the smallest detail could be important." Morgan's fingers drummed anxiously on the bar, her eyes never leaving his face.

"Let me think..." Davis closed his eyes again, taking a deep breath. After a few moments, his eyes opened and met Morgan's gaze. "Woodworking! That's what it was. He was teaching her woodworking, like building furniture and stuff. I remember thinking it was an odd hobby for a pretty young girl."

"Woodworking," Morgan repeated, the word settling heavily in her mind.

Morgan's eyes narrowed, her mind racing as she processed the new information. Woodworking was an unusual hobby for a young woman, especially one who had caught the eye of a man like Joe Dancer. She could sense that this detail would be crucial in finding their next potential victim.

"Thank you, Davis," Morgan said sincerely, her voice firm with determination. "You've given me something valuable to work with."

"Of course, Agent Cross. I hope it helps," Davis replied, a mixture of fear and hope evident in his expression.

As Morgan strode out of the bar, the afternoon sun casting long shadows across the sidewalk, she felt the weight of responsibility settle onto her shoulders. The woodworking detail gnawed at her thoughts, the pieces of the puzzle slowly starting to form a clearer picture. If she could just connect the dots, she might be able to save this girl before it was too late.

With each step, Morgan's resolve hardened. This time, she wouldn't make the same mistakes. This time, she would do whatever it took to bring Joe Dancer to justice and protect the innocent lives he threatened.

But first, she needed to find the connection between this girl and Joe's twisted motives. And she needed to do it fast. Time was not on their side.

***

Back at the precinct, the briefing room was a hive of activity. Thomas and the tech team were hunched over their computers, rapidly typing and scanning through databases as they searched for the identity of the woman with an M name and a woodshop teacher connection.

"Any luck yet?" Morgan asked, striding into the room with urgency in her voice, her eyes darting from one screen to another.

"Nothing concrete so far," Thomas replied, frustration evident in his tone. "We've narrowed it down to a few possible individuals, but we need more information to pinpoint the exact person."

"Keep looking," she urged, her fingers drumming impatiently on the table beside her. "We don't have much time."

As the team continued their search, Morgan paced the room, her mind working overtime to unravel the twisted logic behind Joe's killings. Woodworking seemed like such an innocuous detail, and yet it held the key to saving this girl's life.

"Come on, come on," she muttered, her impatience growing with each passing second. "There has to be something we're missing."

"Wait," Thomas called out suddenly, his fingers flying across the keyboard. "I think I might have something."

Morgan stood by the window, her eyes tracing the movement of the traffic outside, but her focus was on the tense atmosphere within the room. The hum of computer fans and the rapid keystrokes of the tech team were the soundtrack to a high-stakes search for a single piece of information.

"Damn it," she muttered under her breath, biting her thumb in frustration. Her thoughts raced, thinking about how Joe Dancer had slipped through their fingers. She couldn't let him claim another victim.

"Any progress?" Morgan asked, her voice tight as she turned to face Thomas.

"Nothing yet, but we're closing in," one of the analysts replied, his brow furrowed in concentration. "We just need a bit more time."

"Time is something we don't have," Morgan snapped, her anxiety spilling over into anger. She took a deep breath, reminding herself that the team was doing their best.

"Hey, I've got something!" Thomas called out from across the room. Morgan's heart leaped with hope as she crossed the room in two strides, her eyes locked on the screen. Thomas followed suit.

"Talk to me," she said, trying to keep her voice steady.

"Mary Stone, twenty years old," Thomas read from the screen, excitement evident in his voice. "She's enrolled in a woodworking class at the local college. Her teacher is Greg van Sant, a professional woodworker who tutors part-time."

"Finally," Morgan sighed with relief. "Thomas, I want you to go to Mary's address and check things out for yourself. And arrange a team to head to her workplace. Keep me updated on everything, okay?" Morgan instructed, her eyes not leaving the screen.

"Got it," Thomas replied, already grabbing his jacket. He hesitated for a moment before asking, "What are you going to do, Morgan?"

Morgan paused, her mind racing with possibilities. The locations of the murders had all held significance for the victims – the piano hall, the pageant show... It seemed likely that Mary's passion for woodworking would be the key to finding where Joe Dancer had taken her.

"I have an idea," she said, her voice full of determination. "Most of the murder locations were important to the victims. I think Mary's interest in woodworking might lead us to where Joe's taking her."

"Sounds like a solid plan," Thomas nodded. "Be careful, Morgan."

"Always am," she replied, forcing a tight smile as she stood up from the computer. Her heart pounded in her chest, adrenaline coursing through her veins. This was it – the break they'd been waiting for. And she couldn't afford to make any more mistakes.

Just as Morgan reached for the door handle, her fingers inches away from the cool metal, Derik burst into the room, his face flushed and eyes wide with concern. "Morgan, what's happening? What did you find?" he asked, his breaths coming out in short pants.

"Relax, Derik," Morgan said without looking at him, her focus still on the door that led to her next destination. "I've got this covered."

"What do you mean 'you've got this covered'? We're a team, remember?" Derik's voice held an edge of frustration mixed with worry. He knew Morgan had a tendency to take matters into her own hands, but with the stakes so high, they couldn't afford any more missteps.

Morgan sighed, finally meeting his gaze. She saw the fear and determination mirrored in his eyes – emotions she recognized all too well within herself. "Fine," she relented, her voice softening. "I think I know where Joe's taking Mary. You can come with me, but we need to move fast."

"Thank you," Derik replied, relief washing over his features. He followed Morgan out of the room, their footsteps echoing down the empty hallway as they hurried toward the parking lot.

As she slid into the driver's seat, Morgan's grip tightened around the wheel, her knuckles turning white. Images of the victims flashed through her mind, their lifeless bodies a haunting reminder of the danger that loomed ahead. She swallowed hard, trying to push the memories away. Focus, she told herself. You can't save Mary if you're lost in the past.

"Are you sure about this?" Derik asked, breaking the tense silence as they sped through the city streets. "What if it's another dead end?"

"Trust me, Derik," Morgan replied, her voice steady despite the storm of doubts raging inside her. "I've been studying the patterns, and I'm almost certain this is where we'll find Mary."

Derik nodded, his jaw set in a grim line as he stared out the window. They both knew that if Morgan was wrong, they might never get another chance to save Mary – or any other potential victims.

Morgan's heart pounded fiercely against her ribcage, each beat a reminder of the precious time slipping away. She couldn't shake the feeling that every second counted, and she silently prayed that her instincts were right.

"Okay," Derik said, turning back to face her. "Let's do this."

CHAPTER TWENTY NINE

The sun was high, casting bright rays across the manicured lawn as Morgan and Derik climbed the porch steps of Greg van Sant's suburban home. The place oozed normalcy, a façade that Morgan knew concealed an illicit secret. She hesitated for a moment, her hand hovering over the doorbell, then decided against it. Instead, she rapped sharply on the door with her knuckles, the sound echoing through the quiet neighborhood.

"Who is it?" a muffled voice called from inside.

"Open up, we need to talk!" Morgan shouted back, her patience wearing thin.

Greg van Sant's face appeared in the doorway, his eyebrows climbing toward his receding hairline. It was clear he hadn't been expecting visitors, especially not two grim-faced FBI agents.

"Agents Cross and Greene," Morgan said, flashing her badge. "We're here about Mary."

"Mary?" Greg's face drained of color, his eyes widening in alarm. "What about her?"

"Look," Morgan began, cutting straight to the point. "We know about your relationship with Mary. But right now, our priority is her safety. We believe she's in danger, and you might be the only one who can help us find her."

"Mary's in danger?" Greg repeated, the fear in his voice palpable. "What do you mean?"

Greg's face blanched as he stepped onto the porch, hastily closing the door behind him. The faint sound of a television show drifted from inside the house, muffled by the barrier between them. Morgan could tell he was desperate to keep his wife from overhearing their conversation.

"Exactly what are you talking about?" he demanded, his voice barely above a whisper.

"Listen, Mr. van Sant," Morgan replied, her voice low and urgent. "I don't care about your affair with Mary. That's not why we're here. Mary is in imminent danger, and we need to find her before it's too late."

She watched as Greg's eyes widened with fear and disbelief, his breaths coming in short, ragged gasps. Derik stood beside her, his jaw clenched and eyes narrowed, clearly disgusted by the whole situation but keeping his focus on the task at hand.

"Is there anywhere you can think of where she might go? Somewhere personal, somewhere she'd feel safe?" Morgan pressed, feeling the seconds ticking away.

"Safe?" Greg hesitated, his fingers drumming nervously on the doorframe. "I don't... I mean, there is one place..."

"Look, there's no time to explain," Morgan replied urgently, her own worry for the young woman mirrored in her eyes. "We need to know where she might be right now."

Greg hesitated, glancing back towards the closed door as if expecting his wife to burst through it at any moment. He bit his lip, clearly torn between protecting his secret and helping Mary. Finally, he sighed, relenting. "Alright," he said, his voice strained. "There's a place... outside of town. A private woodshop I've been renting. I've taken Mary there for lessons, and sometimes she stays over."

Morgan's heart raced, knowing they needed to act quickly. She forced herself to focus, reminding herself that staying calm was the only way to help Mary now. "Does your wife know about this place?" she asked, even though she could guess the answer.

"No," Greg confirmed, his face flushing with shame. "She doesn't have a clue."

Derik's jaw clenched as he stared at Greg, his expression a mixture of anger and disgust. Morgan could almost feel the tension radiating off him, and she remembered how he had confided in her about his ex-wife's infidelity. That betrayal had left deep wounds, and now Greg's situation was hitting too close to home for Derik.

"Where is this woodshop?" Morgan asked, her tone sharp and urgent. She wanted to get out of there as quickly as possible, not only for Mary's sake but also for Derik's.

Greg fumbled in his pocket for a moment before pulling out a pen and scrap of paper. He jotted down the address, his hand shaking slightly. "Here," he said, handing it to Morgan. "Please, find her."

"Stay here," Morgan commanded, locking eyes with Greg. "We'll do everything we can." She turned on her heel and strode back toward their car, Derik following closely behind.

As they got into the vehicle, she couldn't help but notice Derik's knuckles turning white as he gripped the steering wheel. "You okay?" she asked, concern coloring her voice.

"Fine," he replied curtly, but she knew better. She recognized the pain lurking beneath his terse response. A part of her wanted to reach out, to offer some words of comfort, but she knew that now wasn't the time. They had a job to do.

"Let's get going," Morgan said, her determination steeling her resolve. As the car roared to life, she glanced over at Derik, noticing the way his jaw remained locked, his gaze fixed unerringly on the road ahead. She understood that, for him, this was personal.

Morgan steeled herself for what lay ahead. She focused on the rhythmic beat of her heart, forcing her thoughts to remain centered on their objective. They needed to find Mary before it was too late, and they couldn't afford any distractions—not even the powerful emotions churning inside them.

"Every second counts," she whispered under her breath, her own words serving as a reminder that there was no room for mistakes. As they sped toward the woodshop, Morgan felt an odd mixture of fear and resolve settle in her chest. Somehow, they would save Mary. Failure wasn't an option.

***

The sun blazed high in the sky as Morgan and Derik pulled up to the private woodshop. Its rays pierced through a thin layer of clouds, casting long shadows across the gravel driveway. The building itself was unassuming, its weathered wooden exterior blending seamlessly with the surrounding trees. A car—a nondescript sedan—was parked haphazardly out front, as if abandoned in haste.

"Think that's Mary's car?" Derik asked, peering through the windshield.

"Could be," Morgan replied, her eyes narrowing as she studied the scene. "Stay sharp." She unbuckled her seatbelt and opened the car door, the crunch of gravel beneath her feet punctuating the silence.

Derik followed suit, his gun already drawn as he stepped out onto the uneven ground. Morgan could see the tension radiating off him, and she knew his personal connection to the case was fueling his determination. She drew her own weapon, keeping it at the ready as they approached the building.

"Watch our six," she whispered, her voice barely audible above the rustle of leaves. Derik nodded, his gaze sweeping their surroundings for any signs of danger.

As they neared the entrance to the woodshop, Morgan's heart pounded in her chest, anticipation and fear mingling within her. She took a deep breath, steadying herself before pushing open the door, its hinges creaking in protest.

"Mary?" she called out, her voice echoing off the walls. No response came, just the faint sound of sawdust settling on the floor.

"Clear," Derik said, his focus still on their surroundings. "Let's check inside."

"Right," Morgan agreed, stepping into the dimly lit interior. The smell of freshly cut wood filled her nostrils, accompanied by the pervasive scent of oil and varnish. Her eyes adjusted to the darkness, taking in the various woodworking tools and half-finished projects scattered about the room.

"See anything?" Derik asked, his voice tense as he scanned the space.

"Nothing yet." Morgan's grip tightened on her gun as she moved cautiously through the workshop. Each step felt like an eternity as she searched for any sign of Mary—or Joe Dancer.

"Derik, I need you focused," Morgan thought to herself, hoping he could keep his emotions in check, at least until they found Mary. She knew all too well how personal feelings could cloud judgment, and right now, they couldn't afford any missteps.

"Stay close," she whispered, her pulse quickening with each passing moment. They had to find Mary before it was too late, before Joe Dancer could claim another victim.

And they would—but first, they had to survive whatever lay waiting for them within the depths of the woodshop.

Sunlight cast long, distorted shadows across the workshop as Morgan and Derik moved cautiously around the building. The faint sound of a metallic clanking echoed from somewhere behind the woodshop, causing them to exchange wary glances.

"Did you hear that?" Derik whispered, cocking his head in the direction of the noise.

Morgan nodded, her senses heightened and adrenaline coursing through her veins. "I'll break in and check on Mary. You go see what's making that noise."

"Are you sure splitting up is a good idea?" Derik asked, uncertainty flickering in his eyes.

"Trust me," Morgan replied, her voice firm but reassuring. "Time is running out. We can't risk leaving any stone unturned."

Derik hesitated for a moment before nodding. "Alright. Be careful."

"You too," Morgan said, watching him disappear around the corner before turning her attention back to the task at hand.

With a swift kick, she shattered the door lock and burst into the dimly lit interior of the workshop. Sawdust swirled in the air, dancing in the beams of sunlight that filtered through the grimy windows. Rows of woodworking tools lined the walls, their sharp edges gleaming menacingly in the darkness.

"Mary?!" Morgan called out, her voice tense as she scanned the room. There was no response—only the low hum of an active saw blade growing louder by the second. A feeling of dread crept through her chest, tightening its grip around her heart with each passing moment.

"Come on, where are you?" she muttered under her breath, her eyes darting around the room in search of the young woman.

As she rounded a large workbench, she finally spotted her: Mary, bound and gagged, her gloved hands hooked to a saw belt with the deadly spinning blade drawing closer. Her eyes were wide with terror, tears streaming down her pale cheeks.

"Mary!" Morgan gasped, rushing forward and reaching for the lever that controlled the saw.

CHAPTER THIRTY

Morgan's heart pounded in her ears like a drumbeat as she sprinted towards the saw, the smell of sweat and sawdust filling her nostrils. Her instincts took over, honing in on the lever that would save Mary. Panic surged through her veins as the blade crept closer to the young woman's trembling hands.

Please, God, let me make it in time, Morgan prayed silently.

With one last burst of speed, she reached the lever and yanked it hard. The grinding noise of the saw came to an abrupt halt as the machine shuddered to a stop. Mary collapsed onto the conveyor belt, her body wracked with sobs. Relief washed over Morgan for just a split second before she registered the sound she had dreaded.

A gunshot echoed through the workshop, reverberating off the walls and freezing Morgan's blood in her veins. She spun around, adrenaline surging anew, and found herself staring down the barrel of a gun held by none other than Joe Dancer.

"Joe," Morgan spat, her voice filled with disgust. "You sick bastard."

"Agent Cross," Joe sneered, his eyes cold and devoid of any empathy. "I knew you'd come running."

Morgan fought to keep her fear from showing. She needed to stall him, give Derik a chance to figure out what was happening. Every second counted. "What do you want, Joe? Why involve Mary in this twisted game of yours?"

"Game?" Joe laughed, a chilling sound that sent shivers down Morgan's spine. "This is no game. This is justice."

"Justice?" Morgan scoffed, anger flaring within her. "You think killing innocent women is justice?"

"Innocent?" Joe's grip tightened on the gun, his knuckles turning white. "They were all liars and manipulators. I merely exposed them for who they truly were."

"By taking their lives?" Morgan countered, her voice trembling with rage. "You're the monster here, Joe. Not them." Inside, she was screaming for Derik to hurry, to come to her aid before it was too late.

"Enough!" Joe snarled, his finger twitching on the trigger. "You have no idea what it's like to be betrayed and used, Agent Cross. To have your life ripped apart by someone you trusted."

Morgan's heart pounded in her chest as she stared down the barrel of Joe's gun, its cold menace mirrored in his icy blue eyes. She could see the sweat glistening on his brow even as he fought to keep his expression emotionless.

"Should have stayed out of it, Morgan," Joe growled, his voice barely above a whisper. "You don't understand what I'm doing."

"Enlighten me, then," Morgan challenged, her voice steady despite her racing pulse. "Tell me why you're doing this."

"Simple," he replied, a twisted grin curling his lips. "I'm ridding the world of fakes."

As Joe spoke, Morgan noticed that he was still wearing the gloves she'd seen him with earlier – the same gloves he'd used to deliver his unique brand of 'justice.' She remembered how he'd mentioned a skin condition and wondered if this was more than just a tool for his killings – whether it was part of his motivation.

"Those gloves," she said, trying to keep her tone conversational. "Is that why you chose them? The skin condition?"

"Does it matter?" Joe spat, his grip on the gun tightening. "The gloves are just a means to an end."

"But they mean something to you," Morgan pressed, searching for any glimpse of humanity left within him. "They represent something deeper."

"Enough!" Joe snarled, his finger twitching dangerously on the trigger. "Your attempts at psychoanalysis won't save you now."

Morgan swallowed hard, knowing she was walking a thin line between life and death. She had to find a way to stall him, to give Derik time to reach them. Every second counted.

"Joe," she said softly, allowing her fear to show for the first time. "Whatever pain you've suffered, whatever darkness you've experienced, this isn't the way to make it right. Killing won't heal your wounds."

"Shut up!" he roared, his eyes wild with rage. "You don't know me! You don't know what I've been through!"

"Maybe not," Morgan conceded, her voice still gentle and empathetic. "But I know that there's a part of you that doesn't want to do this. The part that's crying out for help."

For a moment, she thought she saw a flicker of doubt in his eyes, a brief hesitation as he considered her words. But then his expression hardened once more, and the cold, merciless killer returned.

"Too late for that, Agent Cross," Joe whispered, his finger tightening on the trigger. "Far too late."

As the tension in the dimly lit woodshop thickened, Morgan knew she needed to keep Joe talking, to buy time for Derik to come to her aid. The sound of Mary's whimpering and the rhythmic drip of water from a leaking pipe filled the silence between them. Beads of sweat formed on Morgan's brow as she stared down the barrel of Joe's gun, her heart pounding in her ears.

"Joe," she said, her voice steady despite her fear. "Why do you *really* wear the gloves? You're hiding yourself, aren't you?"

His eyes narrowed, but he didn't falter. "I'm not hiding anything, Agent Cross. I need to conceal my skin, or else it will hurt more."

Morgan took a slow, calculated breath, her mind racing to find a way out of this dangerous standoff. She couldn't help but think about how she had let herself become complacent and distracted in recent times. No more mistakes, she promised herself again, even as she feared this one might be her last.

"Does it hurt that much?" she asked, trying to evoke sympathy. "Can't you find another way to cope with your condition without causing harm to others?"

Joe's grip on the gun tightened, his knuckles turning white beneath the fabric of the gloves. "You don't understand," he spat, hatred dripping from his words. "This is my way of taking back control. Of making sure no one else can make me feel weak or powerless ever again."

"Powerful?" Morgan echoed, her tone laced with disbelief. "By killing innocent women? That doesn't make you powerful, Joe. It makes you a coward."

"Shut up!" Joe snarled, teeth gritted as anger flared in his eyes. "You don't know what it feels like to be judged and rejected because of something you can't control!"

But Morgan did know, and she knew that the pain he felt had twisted him into something monstrous. She couldn't let him continue down this dark path, but she was running out of time to stop him.

"Joe," she said, desperately trying to appeal to his humanity. "You don't have to do this. It's not too late to get help, to find a way to heal without hurting others."

"You're wrong, Agent Cross," Joe whispered, cold and unwavering. "It's far too late for me."

Joe's face contorted in fury, his cheeks flushing a deep crimson as he balled his gloved hands into fists. "I'm not a fake!" he screamed, the air around them crackling with tension. "I'm more real than any of those pathetic women I killed!"

Morgan eyed him cautiously, her heart pounding in her chest as she tried to maintain a level-headed demeanor. She could see the raw pain and desperation behind his rage, but that didn't make him any less dangerous.

"Joe," she said softly, attempting to calm him down. "I understand how lonely it must have been for you. To feel like an outcast, judged by others because of something you can't control." She paused for a moment, remembering her own experiences of isolation, both before and during her prison sentence. "But that doesn't give you the right to take lives."

"Lonely?" Joe spat, incredulous. He paced back and forth, his anger escalating with every step. "You think this is about loneliness? This is about justice! Those women got exactly what they deserved!"

As Morgan watched him unravel, she couldn't help but feel a twinge of sympathy for the broken man standing before her. But she also knew that if she didn't stop him now, more innocent lives would be lost.

"Joe," she said firmly, meeting his wild gaze with steady determination. "No amount of pain or loneliness excuses murder. You don't get to decide who deserves to live or die."

"Who are you to tell me what's right and wrong?" Joe snapped, waving his gun menacingly at her. "You're just a washed-up agent, trying to cling to whatever shreds of authority you have left!"

Despite the sting of his words, Morgan refused to let him see her falter. She needed to keep him talking, to buy herself enough time for backup to arrive.

"Maybe I am," she admitted, her voice barely a whisper. "But at least I'm not using my own pain as an excuse to hurt others."

For a moment, Joe seemed taken aback by her response. But the fury in his eyes quickly returned, and Morgan knew that their standoff was far from over.

"Nothing will ever make you understand!" Joe shouted, his hands shaking with rage as he clenched the gun tightly. "I'm doing the world a favor, getting rid of people who don't deserve to be here!"

Morgan took a slow, measured breath, her eyes never leaving Joe's face. She knew that one wrong move could end both their lives in an instant. Her heart pounded in her chest, but she couldn't afford to let fear take over.

"Joe," she said, her voice steady and resolute, "you can't possibly believe that what you're doing is right."

"Right?" He laughed bitterly, a harsh, twisted sound that made Morgan's blood run cold. "You talk about right and wrong like they're absolutes, like anything is black and white. You don't know anything about my life, Agent Cross."

In a sudden, unexpected gesture, Joe ripped off his gloves, revealing malformed hands covered in scarring. Morgan didn't flinch, although it looked very painful. The skin was a mass of angry red welts and scars.

"Look at me!" Joe screamed, waving his grotesque hands in front of her face. "This is what I've had to live with every single day! Do you have any idea what it feels like to be trapped inside a body that betrays you, that makes everyone around you recoil in horror?"

As Morgan stared at Joe's hands, she couldn't let her sympathy for him cloud her judgment. No matter how much pain he'd endured, it didn't justify his actions.

"Joe," she whispered, her voice heavy with empathy, "I'm so sorry for what you've been through. But hurting others won't heal your wounds. It'll only create more suffering for both you and your victims."

"Shut up!" Joe snarled, the gun quivering in his grip. As Morgan watched him struggle with his emotions, her mind raced, searching for a way to resolve the situation without further violence.

She had to make him see reason, to understand that his actions were only causing more harm than good. And she had to do it quickly before either of them made a mistake that could cost them everything.

"Every day of my life, I've had to wear these gloves," Joe gritted his teeth, tears of rage glistening in his eyes. "My skin burns like it's on fire whenever it's exposed to sunlight. And do you know how people react when they see me?" He spat the words out like venom. "With revulsion! Disgust! Especially women who can't bear the thought of being touched by hands like mine."

Morgan could see the anguish etched deep into every line of Joe's face, but she refused to let her resolve waver. His pain was real and raw, but that didn't excuse the atrocities he'd committed.

"Joe, I understand that you've been through hell," she said gently, trying to connect with the broken man before her. "But inflicting that same pain on others isn't going to make your own suffering any less. It's only going to create a cycle of misery."

"Enough!" Joe roared, his face contorted with fury. "You think you're so much better than everyone else, don't you? But you're just as fake as all the rest!"

The gun in his hand trembled as he swung it towards Morgan, and for the first time since their confrontation began, she felt a flicker of fear. She knew what she had to do – find a way to disarm him, both physically and emotionally.

But maybe, it was already too late. Morgan braced herself.

As the barrel of the gun lined up with her chest, time seemed to slow down. Every second stretched into an eternity, and Morgan's heart pounded in her ears like a war drum. She forced herself to remain outwardly calm, even as her mind screamed at her to act.

"Joe," she whispered, her voice steady despite the adrenaline coursing through her veins. "I'm not your enemy. I want to help you. But you have to trust me."

"Trust you?" Joe's laugh was bitter and hollow. "No one has ever given me a reason to trust them. Why should I start now?"

"Because I'm not just anyone," Morgan replied, her gaze never leaving his. "I'm someone who's been through the darkest depths of despair and come out the other side. I know what it's like to feel utterly alone in the world. And I want to make sure that no one else ever has to experience that pain."

"Too late for that," Joe sneered, his finger tightening on the trigger. "You're just as fake as the rest of them, and you need to be stopped."

"Joe, please—" Morgan began, her voice choked with desperation.

But there was no more time for words. The gun roared, and Morgan braced herself for the impact.

Just as the deafening bang of Joe's gunshot shattered the tense silence, the force of another shot reverberated through the woodshop.

Morgan blinked in surprise, feeling no pain. She glanced down to see Joe crumple to the ground, shock and confusion etched on his face.

Derik stood beside him, his gun smoking, and pointed right at him.

He'd stopped him. Morgan let out a breath of relief.

It was over.

CHAPTER THIRTY ONE

The sterile smell of the hospital filled Morgan's nostrils as she sat in the uncomfortable plastic chair of the waiting room. Her hands were balled into fists, knuckles turning white from the pressure. The fluorescent lights above her flickered ever so slightly, casting eerie shadows on the pale blue walls. Memories of her time in prison surfaced unbidden, and she shuddered, trying to push them away.

"Agent Cross?" a nurse called out softly, approaching her with a sympathetic smile.

Morgan looked up, eyes bloodshot from worry. She nodded, unable to muster a response.

"Mary is stable, and she's going to be okay," the nurse informed her gently. "She's resting now, but you can see her when she wakes up."

"Thank you," Morgan whispered, relief washing over her like a wave. She could feel some of the tension leave her body, but the uncertainty about Joe's condition kept her from completely relaxing.

As she sat there, lost in thought, her mind wandered back to that fateful moment when Derik had pulled the trigger. He hadn't wanted to do it, but he'd had no choice. Joe Dancer was a vicious killer, and he'd been inches away from another murder. It had been a split-second decision, and Morgan couldn't help but wonder if things could have gone differently. But at least Mary was safe. Joe's reign of terror was finally over.

"Derik did what he had to do," she murmured to herself, clenching her fists once more. The guilt gnawed at her insides, threatening to consume her. She wished there had been another way to end Joe's spree, but deep down, she knew that there was no reasoning with a man like him.

"Excuse me, are you Agent Cross?" a shaky voice interrupted her thoughts.

Morgan looked up to see a young woman with tear-streaked cheeks holding a worn teddy bear. She recognized her as Mary's sister and nodded.

"Thank you," the young woman whispered, her voice trembling. "For saving my sister."

Morgan reached out and gave her hand a gentle squeeze. Through her own pain, she knew that this was why she had become an agent in the first place: to protect and save vulnerable people like Mary.

"Your sister is strong," Morgan told her softly. "She's going to be okay."

The young woman smiled through her tears, gratitude shining in her eyes. As she walked away, Morgan took a deep breath, trying to find solace in the knowledge that at least one life had been spared from Joe's twisted grasp.

Now, all that was left was to hear Joe's fate – and to face whatever consequences came with it.

The sterile scent of the hospital mixed with the lingering smell of stale coffee as Morgan stared at the floor, her thoughts a whirlwind. The linoleum beneath her feet was worn from years of countless patients and visitors who had walked these halls, each carrying their own burdens. She wondered how many lives had been forever changed within these walls.

"Agent Cross?" a voice called out, pulling Morgan's attention to a doctor standing in the doorway of the waiting room. His face held a mixture of exhaustion and sympathy, his eyes briefly flicking down to the clipboard he held.

"Joe Dancer," she replied, her voice steady despite the rapid beating of her heart.

"I'm sorry, Agent Cross," he said, hesitating for a moment before continuing. "He didn't make it. The bullet caused too much damage."

Morgan's chest tightened, a mixture of relief and regret washing over her. She shifted in her seat, her legs suddenly feeling weak. "Thank you, Doctor," she managed to say, her voice barely audible.

Morgan looked into the doctor's eyes, searching for any hint of hope. His solemn expression, however, told her everything she needed to know. With a heavy heart, she nodded and managed a weak smile. "Thank you, doctor, for trying." Her voice was barely a whisper, but it carried all the gratitude she could muster.

"Of course," he replied, giving her a small, sympathetic smile before retreating down the hallway. Morgan watched him go, then turned toward the exit. The sterile white walls seemed to close in on her as she walked, each step bringing her closer to the warm embrace of the night outside.

As the automatic doors slid open, Morgan stepped out into the balmy air. The scent of freshly cut grass mingled with the distant hum of traffic, momentarily grounding her in a semblance of normalcy. She took a deep breath, savoring the sensation of life pulsing through her veins – something Joe Dancer would never experience again.

"Hey." A familiar voice pulled her from her thoughts.

"Derik." She turned to see her partner standing nearby, his usually stoic features marred by grief. His green eyes shimmered with unshed tears, making him look more vulnerable than she had ever seen him before.

"Is it true?" Derik asked, his voice cracking slightly under the weight of his emotions. "Did Joe…?"

Morgan hesitated, wishing she could spare him this pain. But they were partners, and the truth always came first. "No," she admitted, lowering her gaze. "He didn't make it."

"Damn it." Derik's shoulders slumped, as though the weight of the world had just crashed down upon him. He rubbed a hand over his face, visibly struggling to maintain his composure.

Morgan wanted to comfort him, but she knew that her own emotions were too raw to offer any solace. Instead, she focused on the sensation of her heart pounding in her chest, reminding herself that she was alive and had a duty to keep fighting for justice. Joe Dancer's life might have ended, but hers would continue – even if it meant shouldering the burden of guilt and grief.

Morgan observed Derik as he stood there, his tall frame slumped and defeated. The fluorescent glow of the streetlights illuminated the trails of tears streaking down his face, making his green eyes appear even more haunted than usual. Concern washed over her, and she couldn't help but ask, "Derik, why are you so upset? I mean, I know it's not easy, but you've had to kill on duty before."

He sighed, running a hand through his disheveled hair. "I know, Morgan. It's just... I never like killing, no matter the circumstances. And with everything so bad between us, it's just a lot." He looked away, his gaze settling on a crumpled beer can in the corner of the parking lot. "I'm trying really hard not to drink right now."

Morgan's heart twisted, understanding the weight of his struggle. She knew all too well how much he relied on alcohol to numb the pain. In that moment, she saw the vulnerability in him – a vulnerability that mirrored her own.

"Derik," she started gently, placing a hand on his shoulder, feeling the tension beneath her touch. "I know we have our issues, but right now, we need to focus on what we can control. We stopped Joe from hurting anyone else, and that counts for something."

His eyes locked onto hers, searching for reassurance. "But at what cost, Morgan? A man is dead because of me."

She squeezed his shoulder, holding his gaze. "You did what you had to do. Don't let Joe's actions define your worth."

Derik swallowed hard, nodding as he processed her words. Around them, the night air hummed with the distant sounds of traffic and life continuing beyond their bubble of sorrow. He took a deep breath, steadying himself, and slowly straightened up.

"Thanks, Morgan," he said quietly, his voice wavering.

Morgan hesitated before she spoke, watching Derik's despondent posture. "You need to go home and get some rest, Derik," she said firmly. "And for God's sake, don't drink."

"Right..." he replied, his voice hoarse with unshed tears. He flashed a weak smile that didn't quite reach his eyes. "Take care of yourself, Morgan."

"Likewise," she managed, her heart aching as she watched him walk away into the night.

EPILOGUE

Later that evening, Morgan found herself on her couch, buried beneath a soft blanket. Skunk, her loyal Pitbull, lay beside her, his warm body pressed against hers. The comforting weight of him seemed to be the only thing keeping her grounded in the moment.

Her thoughts drifted back to Derik, his tear-filled eyes haunting her. She couldn't deny that she cared about him, but she couldn't be his emotional support when she was still struggling with her own demons. It wasn't fair to either of them.

"Skunk," she whispered, stroking his soft fur, "I have to stay strong. I can't let myself get tangled up in someone else's problems when I'm barely holding it together myself."

Skunk lifted his head, his dark eyes meeting hers as if he understood the gravity of her words. He let out a quiet huff and nuzzled closer to her, offering silent comfort.

"Thanks, buddy," she murmured, her hand continuing its gentle path through his fur. "You always know how to make me feel better."

The room was filled with the faint hum of the television, background noise meant to drown out the emptiness that threatened to engulf her. Images flickered across the screen, but she paid them no mind, her thoughts consumed by the events of the day.

She knew that tomorrow would bring new challenges, new obstacles to overcome. But for now, she would allow herself this moment of peace, wrapped in the warmth of her companion and the familiar scent of home.

The low hum of the television filled the room, casting a dim glow on Skunk's sleeping form. Morgan stared at the flickering screen, but her thoughts were elsewhere - mulling over her conversation with Derik and the emotional weight it carried. She absently stroked Skunk's fur, finding comfort in his warmth beside her.

Her phone buzzed on the coffee table, cutting through her thoughts. She glanced at the screen, her lips curving into a small, genuine smile for the first time that day. It was Thomas.

"Hey, Thomas," she answered, her voice softening. "It's good to hear from you."

"Hey, Morgan," he replied, the sound of his voice like a balm for her frayed nerves. "I've got some news. I managed to hack into the FBI database you mentioned, and I think I might know something about who framed you."

Morgan's heart raced at his words, hope surging within her. She tightened her grip on the phone, her knuckles turning white.

"Tell me everything," she urged, her voice barely above a whisper.

"Unfortunately, I can't discuss this over the phone, but I promise you, it's big."

Morgan leaned forward, a smile playing at her lips. "How big are we talking?"

***

Thomas leaned back on his couch, the darkness of his apartment cloaking him like a protective shroud. He took a slow sip from his glass, letting the burn of the whiskey mingle with the coldness of the ice cubes. The amber liquid shimmered in the faint light that found its way through the closed blinds.

"Listen, Morgan," he said, his voice low and cautious as it carried over the phone. "I've got something you're going to want to hear, but I can't tell you over the phone. It's too risky."

Morgan's eagerness was palpable even through the line. "Do you want to meet up then?" she asked, her usual stoicism giving way to hope.

"Of course," Thomas replied, his fingers idly tracing the condensation on his glass. "Not tonight, though. Tomorrow, for sure."

"Where should we meet?" Her question was laced with anticipation, and Thomas could almost see her mind racing with the possibilities.

"I'll let you know tomorrow. I'm not sure what work is gonna demand of me. You know how it is."

"I do. Thank you, really," Morgan's voice reached him through the phone, gratitude evident in her tone. "I don't know what I'd do without you."

"Hey, it's what I'm here for." Thomas grinned, his eyes narrowing playfully in the darkness. "But I expect a second date after all this is over, Cross."

Morgan laughed, a genuine sound that made Thomas's heart swell with pride. "You've got yourself a deal, Thomas Grady."

"Good," he replied, his smile still lingering as he ended the call.

The moment the line went dead, Thomas's expression shifted. The warmth drained from his face, replaced by a cold, calculating stare. He took a slow, deliberate sip of his whiskey, the burn in his throat doing nothing to bring the warmth back to his eyes.

As the liquid fire settled into his stomach, his thoughts turned inward. The information he held could crack open the case and bring justice to those who had wronged Morgan, but it also carried great risk. He knew the cost of playing with fire, and yet, here he was, stoking the flames.

The amber liquid swirled in the glass, casting a warm glow against the stark darkness of Thomas's apartment. He stared at it for a moment, his thoughts racing, before setting the whiskey down on the coffee table with a soft clink. Every muscle in his body tensed as he prepared himself for what came next.

His thumb hovered over the screen of his phone, hesitating for only a second before pressing down on the contact labeled "Boss" and bringing the device to his ear. The line rang once, twice, and then clicked as the call connected.

"Thomas," said the man on the other end, his voice deep and authoritative. "What do you have for me?"

"Everything's going according to plan," Thomas replied, his tone cold and detached. His mind flashed back to the warmth of Morgan's laugh, but he pushed it aside, focusing instead on the task at hand. "I've got Morgan Cross right where we need her. It's only a matter of time now."

"Good," the man responded, his voice betraying no emotion. "You know how important this is. We can't afford any mistakes."

"Understood," Thomas said, his jaw clenched as he fought to keep his emotions in check. He couldn't let his boss sense even a hint of doubt or hesitation – not when so much was at stake.

"Keep me updated," the man ordered. "And remember, Thomas – you're playing a dangerous game here. Don't get too attached. This is business, nothing more."

Thomas swallowed hard, suppressing the urge to lash out. Instead, he forced himself to maintain his icy façade. "Of course," he said, teeth gritted. "I won't disappoint you."

"See that you don't," the man replied, and the line went dead.

NOW AVAILABLE!

FOR NOW
(A Morgan Cross FBI Suspense Thriller—Book Seven)

A string of victims found with the same eerie trademark—fake teeth planted in their mouth. An ex-con FBI agent, unchained, and willing to stop at nothing. And a diabolical killer to match….

"A masterpiece of thriller and mystery."
—Books and Movie Reviews, Roberto Mattos (re Once Gone)

FOR NOW is book #7 in a long-anticipated new series by #1 bestseller and USA Today bestselling author Blake Pierce, whose bestseller Once Gone (a free download) has received over 7,000 five star ratings and reviews.

Superstar FBI Agent Morgan Cross was at the height of her career when she was framed, wrongly imprisoned, and sent to do 10 hard years in prison. Finally exonerated and set free, Morgan emerges from jail as a changed person—hardened, ruthless, closed off to the world, and unsure how to start again. When the FBI comes knocking, desperately needing Morgan to return and hunt down a killer who seems to be obsessed with drowning, Morgan is torn.

Morgan is not the same person, no longer willing to play by the rules, and will stop at nothing this time. In a non-stop thriller, it will be a deadly cat and mouse chase between a diabolical killer and an ex-con FBI agent who has nothing left to lose—with a new victim's fate riding on it all.

A page-turning and harrowing crime thriller featuring a brilliant and tortured FBI agent, the Morgan Cross series is a riveting mystery, packed with non-stop action, suspense, twists and turns, revelations, and driven by a breakneck pace that will keep you flipping pages late into the night. Fans of Rachel Caine, Teresa Driscoll and Robert Dugoni are sure to fall in love.

Future books in the series will be available soon!

"An edge of your seat thriller in a new series that keeps you turning pages! ...So many twists, turns and red herrings… I can't wait to see what happens next."
—Reader review (Her Last Wish)

"A strong, complex story about two FBI agents trying to stop a serial killer. If you want an author to capture your attention and have you guessing, yet trying to put the pieces together, Pierce is your author!"
—Reader review (Her Last Wish)

"A typical Blake Pierce twisting, turning, roller coaster ride suspense thriller. Will have you turning the pages to the last sentence of the last chapter!!!"
—Reader review (City of Prey)

"Right from the start we have an unusual protagonist that I haven't seen done in this genre before. The action is nonstop… A very atmospheric novel that will keep you turning pages well into the wee hours."
—Reader review (City of Prey)

"Everything that I look for in a book… a great plot, interesting characters, and grabs your interest right away. The book moves along at a breakneck pace and stays that way until the end. Now on go I to book two!"
—Reader review (Girl, Alone)

"Exciting, heart pounding, edge of your seat book… a must read for mystery and suspense readers!"
—Reader review (Girl, Alone)

Blake Pierce

Blake Pierce is the USA Today bestselling author of the RILEY PAGE mystery series, which includes seventeen books. Blake Pierce is also the author of the MACKENZIE WHITE mystery series, comprising fourteen books; of the AVERY BLACK mystery series, comprising six books; of the KERI LOCKE mystery series, comprising five books; of the MAKING OF RILEY PAIGE mystery series, comprising six books; of the KATE WISE mystery series, comprising seven books; of the CHLOE FINE psychological suspense mystery, comprising six books; of the JESSIE HUNT psychological suspense thriller series, comprising thirty-one books; of the AU PAIR psychological suspense thriller series, comprising three books; of the ZOE PRIME mystery series, comprising six books; of the ADELE SHARP mystery series, comprising sixteen books, of the EUROPEAN VOYAGE cozy mystery series, comprising six books; of the LAURA FROST FBI suspense thriller, comprising eleven books; of the ELLA DARK FBI suspense thriller, comprising twenty-one books (and counting); of the A YEAR IN EUROPE cozy mystery series, comprising nine books, of the AVA GOLD mystery series, comprising six books; of the RACHEL GIFT mystery series, comprising thirteen books (and counting); of the VALERIE LAW mystery series, comprising nine books (and counting); of the PAIGE KING mystery series, comprising eight books (and counting); of the MAY MOORE mystery series, comprising eleven books; of the CORA SHIELDS mystery series, comprising eight books (and counting); of the NICKY LYONS mystery series, comprising eight books (and counting), of the CAMI LARK mystery series, comprising nine books (and counting), of the AMBER YOUNG mystery series, comprising seven books (and counting), of the DAISY FORTUNE mystery series, comprising five books (and counting), of the FIONA RED mystery series, comprising nine books (and counting), of the FAITH BOLD mystery series, comprising eight books (and counting), of the JULIETTE HART mystery series, comprising five books (and counting), of the MORGAN CROSS mystery series, comprising seven books (and counting), and of the new FINN WRIGHT mystery series, comprising five books (and counting).

An avid reader and lifelong fan of the mystery and thriller genres,

Blake loves to hear from you, so please feel free to visit www.blakepierceauthor.com to learn more and stay in touch.

LET HER GO (Book #1)
LET HER BE (Book #2)
LET HER HOPE (Book #3)
LET HER WISH (Book #4)
LET HER LIVE (Book #5)
LET HER RUN (Book #6)
LET HER HIDE (Book #7)
LET HER BELIEVE (Book #8)
LET HER FORGET (Book #9)

DAISY FORTUNE MYSTERY SERIES
NEED YOU (Book #1)
CLAIM YOU (Book #2)
CRAVE YOU (Book #3)
CHOOSE YOU (Book #4)
CHASE YOU (Book #5)

AMBER YOUNG MYSTERY SERIES
ABSENT PITY (Book #1)
ABSENT REMORSE (Book #2)
ABSENT FEELING (Book #3)
ABSENT MERCY (Book #4)
ABSENT REASON (Book #5)
ABSENT SANITY (Book #6)
ABSENT LIFE (Book #7)

CAMI LARK MYSTERY SERIES
JUST ME (Book #1)
JUST OUTSIDE (Book #2)
JUST RIGHT (Book #3)
JUST FORGET (Book #4)
JUST ONCE (Book #5)
JUST HIDE (Book #6)
JUST NOW (Book #7)
JUST HOPE (Book #8)
JUST LEAVE (Book #9)

NICKY LYONS MYSTERY SERIES
ALL MINE (Book #1)
ALL HIS (Book #2)

ALL HE SEES (Book #3)
ALL ALONE (Book #4)
ALL FOR ONE (Book #5)
ALL HE TAKES (Book #6)
ALL FOR ME (Book #7)
ALL IN (Book #8)

CORA SHIELDS MYSTERY SERIES
UNDONE (Book #1)
UNWANTED (Book #2)
UNHINGED (Book #3)
UNSAID (Book #4)
UNGLUED (Book #5)
UNSTABLE (Book #6)
UNKNOWN (Book #7)
UNAWARE (Book #8)

MAY MOORE SUSPENSE THRILLER
NEVER RUN (Book #1)
NEVER TELL (Book #2)
NEVER LIVE (Book #3)
NEVER HIDE (Book #4)
NEVER FORGIVE (Book #5)
NEVER AGAIN (Book #6)
NEVER LOOK BACK (Book #7)
NEVER FORGET (Book #8)
NEVER LET GO (Book #9)
NEVER PRETEND (Book #10)
NEVER HESITATE (Book #11)

PAIGE KING MYSTERY SERIES
THE GIRL HE PINED (Book #1)
THE GIRL HE CHOSE (Book #2)
THE GIRL HE TOOK (Book #3)
THE GIRL HE WISHED (Book #4)
THE GIRL HE CROWNED (Book #5)
THE GIRL HE WATCHED (Book #6)
THE GIRL HE WANTED (Book #7)
THE GIRL HE CLAIMED (Book #8)

VALERIE LAW MYSTERY SERIES
NO MERCY (Book #1)
NO PITY (Book #2)
NO FEAR (Book #3)
NO SLEEP (Book #4)
NO QUARTER (Book #5)
NO CHANCE (Book #6)
NO REFUGE (Book #7)
NO GRACE (Book #8)
NO ESCAPE (Book #9)

RACHEL GIFT MYSTERY SERIES
HER LAST WISH (Book #1)
HER LAST CHANCE (Book #2)
HER LAST HOPE (Book #3)
HER LAST FEAR (Book #4)
HER LAST CHOICE (Book #5)
HER LAST BREATH (Book #6)
HER LAST MISTAKE (Book #7)
HER LAST DESIRE (Book #8)
HER LAST REGRET (Book #9)
HER LAST HOUR (Book #10)
HER LAST SHOT (Book #11)
HER LAST PRAYER (Book #12)
HER LAST LIE (Book #13)

AVA GOLD MYSTERY SERIES
CITY OF PREY (Book #1)
CITY OF FEAR (Book #2)
CITY OF BONES (Book #3)
CITY OF GHOSTS (Book #4)
CITY OF DEATH (Book #5)
CITY OF VICE (Book #6)

A YEAR IN EUROPE
A MURDER IN PARIS (Book #1)
DEATH IN FLORENCE (Book #2)
VENGEANCE IN VIENNA (Book #3)
A FATALITY IN SPAIN (Book #4)

ELLA DARK FBI SUSPENSE THRILLER
GIRL, ALONE (Book #1)
GIRL, TAKEN (Book #2)
GIRL, HUNTED (Book #3)
GIRL, SILENCED (Book #4)
GIRL, VANISHED (Book 5)
GIRL ERASED (Book #6)
GIRL, FORSAKEN (Book #7)
GIRL, TRAPPED (Book #8)
GIRL, EXPENDABLE (Book #9)
GIRL, ESCAPED (Book #10)
GIRL, HIS (Book #11)
GIRL, LURED (Book #12)
GIRL, MISSING (Book #13)
GIRL, UNKNOWN (Book #14)
GIRL, DECEIVED (Book #15)
GIRL, FORLORN (Book #16)
GIRL, REMADE (Book #17)
GIRL, BETRAYED (Book #18)
GIRL, BOUND (Book #19)
GIRL, REFORMED (Book #20)
GIRL, REBORN (Book #21)

LAURA FROST FBI SUSPENSE THRILLER
ALREADY GONE (Book #1)
ALREADY SEEN (Book #2)
ALREADY TRAPPED (Book #3)
ALREADY MISSING (Book #4)
ALREADY DEAD (Book #5)
ALREADY TAKEN (Book #6)
ALREADY CHOSEN (Book #7)
ALREADY LOST (Book #8)
ALREADY HIS (Book #9)
ALREADY LURED (Book #10)
ALREADY COLD (Book #11)

EUROPEAN VOYAGE COZY MYSTERY SERIES
MURDER (AND BAKLAVA) (Book #1)
DEATH (AND APPLE STRUDEL) (Book #2)
CRIME (AND LAGER) (Book #3)

MISFORTUNE (AND GOUDA) (Book #4)
CALAMITY (AND A DANISH) (Book #5)
MAYHEM (AND HERRING) (Book #6)

ADELE SHARP MYSTERY SERIES
LEFT TO DIE (Book #1)
LEFT TO RUN (Book #2)
LEFT TO HIDE (Book #3)
LEFT TO KILL (Book #4)
LEFT TO MURDER (Book #5)
LEFT TO ENVY (Book #6)
LEFT TO LAPSE (Book #7)
LEFT TO VANISH (Book #8)
LEFT TO HUNT (Book #9)
LEFT TO FEAR (Book #10)
LEFT TO PREY (Book #11)
LEFT TO LURE (Book #12)
LEFT TO CRAVE (Book #13)
LEFT TO LOATHE (Book #14)
LEFT TO HARM (Book #15)
LEFT TO RUIN (Book #16)

THE AU PAIR SERIES
ALMOST GONE (Book#1)
ALMOST LOST (Book #2)
ALMOST DEAD (Book #3)

ZOE PRIME MYSTERY SERIES
FACE OF DEATH (Book#1)
FACE OF MURDER (Book #2)
FACE OF FEAR (Book #3)
FACE OF MADNESS (Book #4)
FACE OF FURY (Book #5)
FACE OF DARKNESS (Book #6)

A JESSIE HUNT PSYCHOLOGICAL SUSPENSE SERIES
THE PERFECT WIFE (Book #1)
THE PERFECT BLOCK (Book #2)
THE PERFECT HOUSE (Book #3)
THE PERFECT SMILE (Book #4)

THE PERFECT LIE (Book #5)
THE PERFECT LOOK (Book #6)
THE PERFECT AFFAIR (Book #7)
THE PERFECT ALIBI (Book #8)
THE PERFECT NEIGHBOR (Book #9)
THE PERFECT DISGUISE (Book #10)
THE PERFECT SECRET (Book #11)
THE PERFECT FAÇADE (Book #12)
THE PERFECT IMPRESSION (Book #13)
THE PERFECT DECEIT (Book #14)
THE PERFECT MISTRESS (Book #15)
THE PERFECT IMAGE (Book #16)
THE PERFECT VEIL (Book #17)
THE PERFECT INDISCRETION (Book #18)
THE PERFECT RUMOR (Book #19)
THE PERFECT COUPLE (Book #20)
THE PERFECT MURDER (Book #21)
THE PERFECT HUSBAND (Book #22)
THE PERFECT SCANDAL (Book #23)
THE PERFECT MASK (Book #24)
THE PERFECT RUSE (Book #25)
THE PERFECT VENEER (Book #26)
THE PERFECT PEOPLE (Book #27)
THE PERFECT WITNESS (Book #28)
THE PERFECT APPEARANCE (Book #29)
THE PERFECT TRAP (Book #30)
THE PERFECT EXPRESSION (Book #31)

CHLOE FINE PSYCHOLOGICAL SUSPENSE SERIES
NEXT DOOR (Book #1)
A NEIGHBOR'S LIE (Book #2)
CUL DE SAC (Book #3)
SILENT NEIGHBOR (Book #4)
HOMECOMING (Book #5)
TINTED WINDOWS (Book #6)

KATE WISE MYSTERY SERIES
IF SHE KNEW (Book #1)
IF SHE SAW (Book #2)
IF SHE RAN (Book #3)

IF SHE HID (Book #4)
IF SHE FLED (Book #5)
IF SHE FEARED (Book #6)
IF SHE HEARD (Book #7)

THE MAKING OF RILEY PAIGE SERIES
WATCHING (Book #1)
WAITING (Book #2)
LURING (Book #3)
TAKING (Book #4)
STALKING (Book #5)
KILLING (Book #6)

RILEY PAIGE MYSTERY SERIES
ONCE GONE (Book #1)
ONCE TAKEN (Book #2)
ONCE CRAVED (Book #3)
ONCE LURED (Book #4)
ONCE HUNTED (Book #5)
ONCE PINED (Book #6)
ONCE FORSAKEN (Book #7)
ONCE COLD (Book #8)
ONCE STALKED (Book #9)
ONCE LOST (Book #10)
ONCE BURIED (Book #11)
ONCE BOUND (Book #12)
ONCE TRAPPED (Book #13)
ONCE DORMANT (Book #14)
ONCE SHUNNED (Book #15)
ONCE MISSED (Book #16)
ONCE CHOSEN (Book #17)

MACKENZIE WHITE MYSTERY SERIES
BEFORE HE KILLS (Book #1)
BEFORE HE SEES (Book #2)
BEFORE HE COVETS (Book #3)
BEFORE HE TAKES (Book #4)
BEFORE HE NEEDS (Book #5)
BEFORE HE FEELS (Book #6)
BEFORE HE SINS (Book #7)

BEFORE HE HUNTS (Book #8)
BEFORE HE PREYS (Book #9)
BEFORE HE LONGS (Book #10)
BEFORE HE LAPSES (Book #11)
BEFORE HE ENVIES (Book #12)
BEFORE HE STALKS (Book #13)
BEFORE HE HARMS (Book #14)

AVERY BLACK MYSTERY SERIES
CAUSE TO KILL (Book #1)
CAUSE TO RUN (Book #2)
CAUSE TO HIDE (Book #3)
CAUSE TO FEAR (Book #4)
CAUSE TO SAVE (Book #5)
CAUSE TO DREAD (Book #6)

KERI LOCKE MYSTERY SERIES
A TRACE OF DEATH (Book #1)
A TRACE OF MURDER (Book #2)
A TRACE OF VICE (Book #3)
A TRACE OF CRIME (Book #4)
A TRACE OF HOPE (Book #5)

Made in the USA
Coppell, TX
15 March 2024

30156911R00094